"Evenin', ladies. Seems y'all left somethin' behind."

The women spun around with weapons raised. Andria had snatched up a nearby log, while Bella had her rifle trained on him.

"Whoa, it's just me!" Duncan raised his arms.

They stood and stared at him for a few moments before recognizing him and lowering the weapons. Bella leaned against hers and glowered while Andria stood with a hand to her heart. Andria looked as if she'd seen a ghost while Bella returned his cocky glance and looked over at their belongings. "I don't see anything of importance missin', Andria, do you? Whatever could we have forgotten, Reverend Bowers?"

"Me."

Bella rolled her eyes. "In order to 'forget' you, I would have had to plan to bring you along in the first place. In case you didn't notice, I didn't plan any such thing."

PAIGE WINSHIP DOOLY is the author of over a dozen books and novellas. She enjoys living in the coastal Deep South with her family, after having grown up in the sometimes extremely cold Midwest. She is happily married to her high school sweetheart and loves their life of adventure in a full house with six homeschooled children and two dogs.

Books by Paige Winship Dooly

HEARTSONG PRESENTS
HP84—Heart's Desire
HP775—Treasure in the Hills
HP807—The Greatest Find
HP820—Carousel Dreams
HP840—The Petticoat Doctor
HP903—The Lightkeeper's Daughter
HP924—The Displaced Belle

Don't miss out on any of our super romances. Write to us at the following address for information on our newest releases and club information.

Heartsong Presents Readers' Service
PO Box 721
Uhrichsville, OH 44683

Or visit www.heartsongpresents.com

The Reluctant Outlaw

Paige Winship Dooly

Heartsong Presents

To my good friend Jennifer Sexton. It isn't often that a friendship lasts through the decades. I'm so glad to have you as that kind of friend!

A note from the Author:
I love to hear from my readers! You may correspond with me by writing:

Paige Winship Dooly
Author Relations
PO Box 721
Uhrichsville, OH 44683

ISBN 978-1-61626-241-9

THE RELUCTANT OUTLAW

All scripture quotations are taken from the King James Version of the Bible.

All of the characters and events in this book are fictitious. Any resemblance to actual persons, living or dead, or to actual events is purely coincidental.

Our mission is to publish and distribute inspirational products offering exceptional value and biblical encouragement to the masses.

PRINTED IN THE U.S.A.

one

North Georgia Mountains, 1873

Bella narrowed her eyes and resisted the urge to turn the squint into a full-fledged glare as her arrogant brother rode his horse back and forth on the hard-packed ground in front of her. It wouldn't serve any purpose to make him mad. The corner of her mouth turned up in a hard smile. He was already halfway to mad, much like their deceased father, and because of that she didn't need to make him angry. She forced her mouth into a straight line and focused on the tufts of dust that rose into the air from Wayne's huge horse's prancing. She tried hard to control her anger. She didn't want to be like them. She wanted out. She no longer wanted to be part of her brothers' gang. She never had wanted to be part of it, not that her opinion had ever been asked.

Bella sat high in her saddle listening to Wayne's lecture, determined to hold her ground. His eyes gleamed in a fanatical way, one she'd come to recognize as a prelude to a tangent, his stature full of self-importance. His moods were becoming more unpredictable every day. Bella refused to let him get to her. She'd had it with his attempts at intimidation. Her brother was most definitely turning into a madman. Or maybe he already was one. With her rough family history, at least after her mother passed away, it was difficult to tell.

"You *girls*"—Wayne accentuated the term with syrupy contempt, wanting Bella and her younger sister, Andria, to know their place—"need to ride down the mountain today. Be prepared to go into town tomorrow at first light. Don't dally, and don't draw attention to yourselves. I want you to check around and see if they're gettin' ready to send another posse up here anytime soon."

Charlie, the older brother closest to Bella in age, snorted.

Wayne swung around to face him. "You got a problem with something I said, Charlie?"

"There ain't no way these two are gonna go into town and not draw attention. You happen to look at 'em lately? I mean *really* look at 'em?"

Wayne stared from Bella to Andria and back again. "They look all right to me."

"They look more than all right, Wayne. They ain't little girls no more. Them single men in town will take one look and will be after them to stay. Fights'll break out in their wake. I've seen it happen with plainer women, and these two ain't plain."

Wayne sneered. "Well, they *ain't gonna* stay on—you hear that, Bella? Andria? You won't be stayin' in town. You get in there, do your business, and get out."

Bella heard all right. Staying in town was the last thing she wanted. "I hardly plan to ride into town and get myself hitched, Wayne. Settlin' down with any man is the last thing on my mind."

Her father and brothers made that decision easy. As far as she was concerned, she'd stay unhitched forever if the concept meant being tied up for life with a man who resembled the likes of her brothers. And since she'd never before seen a man who acted otherwise, she had no intention of getting hitched at all. Ever.

Bella's secret wish was to be a schoolteacher, but she doubted that would ever happen. Single women were preferred when it came to teaching, so the arrangement would be just about perfect. She doubted any school would hire a member of one of the most notorious outlaw gangs in the area, but she could always dream. Her participation in the gang might be reluctant on her end, but no one would see it that way if they were caught.

Wayne continued his lecture. "Good. No weddin's for either of you, and don't you forget it." Wayne rode closer and leaned into Bella's face. She could feel the brim of his hat against her forehead as he stared into her soul with empty, hard eyes. "Speakin' of, what *is* on your mind, little sister? You been awfully quiet these past few days. You better not be thinkin' about tryin' somethin'."

Bella met his gaze for several long moments before deciding it was best not to answer him. She was thinking of trying something all right, but she wasn't about to tell Wayne that. And she refused to tell a lie, even to the likes of him. She raised an eyebrow and lifted one shoulder before turning her horse away from him.

Before she could move away, Wayne hit her hard from behind, knocking her from her place on the saddle. "Don't *ever* turn your back on me, you hear?"

The motion swept her sideways, and though she grasped for a hold on the saddle horn, she lost her grip and arced through the air.

Andria screamed as Bella sprawled flat on her back on the hard, dusty ground. Everything faded to black, though Bella could still hear the horses as they shuffled their hooves nervously beside her, far too close to her head. She panicked when she realized she couldn't pull a breath into her lungs. She fought to take in air. She couldn't die like this—not now. Andria needed her.

"Now look what you've gone and done!" Charlie yelled as he swung down from his own mount and knelt at her side. Bella felt his knee brush against her as he gingerly tilted her up into his arms. "She can't breathe. You done broke her back, you stupid idiot!"

"Her back ain't broke. I just knocked the wind out of her." Wayne spat a thread of tobacco. From the sound of it, the disgusting substance landed mere inches from Bella's face.

Charlie shifted her again, and fresh air gushed into Bella's lungs. She took a deep draw of the life-sustaining air before giving in to the anger that simmered deep inside. Her vision cleared, and she located Wayne. He remained where he was, straddling his horse, but now he leaned forward, one arm resting cockily on his thigh as he peered down at her with a hateful smirk on his face. She pushed up and lunged for him. "How—dare—you—"

Charlie held her back. "Not now, Bella. Let it go."

His words were quiet, for her ears only.

Her breath came in short, fast bursts as she watched Wayne ride away. He glanced back over his shoulder, and she fought again, futilely, against Charlie's hold.

Inappropriate humor danced in Wayne's eyes as he surveyed her. After a brief moment, he emotionally discarded her with an expression of disdain. He pulled his hat low on his forehead, a defensive move that cast his eyes into dark shadowed orbs. Bella shivered.

"Remember, ride in. Ride out. Don't draw attention. Attend to business and return home. That's an order."

"You might as well order the wind to stop blowing. Like Charlie said, we can't help but draw attention." Bella hissed the words, not caring if he heard or not. "How often do you think two mountain women ride alone into that tiny ole town?"

Wayne either didn't hear her or chose to ignore her statements. "See ya when you get back. I'll be waitin'." He slowly turned his horse and rode toward the high trail that looked out over the valley.

Bella watched him go. Wayne had reached a new low when he'd knocked her from the saddle.

"I hate him, Charlie." Bella felt something crack deep inside as she uttered the statement. "I hate him."

Pain stabbed through her heart as she stated the words. She'd never felt such wrath, hadn't ever hated anyone before now. She'd hated circumstances and situations, she'd hated certain days and experiences, but never had she hated another person with such passion. The realization scared her. If she continued on this path, she'd end up as mean and full of hate as Wayne. She had to get out of the gang, and she needed to take her younger sister with her.

Charlie scratched his head in frustration. "Bella, you gotta speak to Wayne with respect from now on. This new attitude of yours ain't gonna do no one no good."

"I'm the one with a new attitude?" Bella asked, incredulous. "Did you see what Wayne just did to me? *He's* the one who's out of control."

Concern filled Charlie's eyes. He was no saint, but he wasn't as bad as Wayne. "Ain't gonna do no good if you keep challengin' him, Belle. You just gotta do as he says."

She'd do nothing of the kind, but she wouldn't admit that to Charlie. He was in too deep and fully under his older brother's control.

"I understand, Charlie."

"I hope you do. He ain't stable right now."

He hasn't been stable in a long, long time.

A short time later, Bella thought about Charlie's comment as she guided her horse down the steep mountain trail at as fast a pace as she dared. She was still filled with anger—anger that Wayne had ignited deep inside her. *Stable, hmph.* Wayne hadn't been stable since as far back as she could remember. Even when their mother had been alive, Bella could remember him challenging her every request. Many times Bella had seen fear move into the gentle-natured woman's eyes when she'd attempted to reprimand her son. To Bella's recollection, Wayne had never been anything near stable.

Even though Bella was angry, she still proceeded down the mountain with a heightened level of awareness. She knew the pitfalls that could await her and her sister on the unseen parts of the path. They moved stealthily with purpose, yet also with caution. Her brother wasn't the only weasel who lived and rode in these mountains.

The path widened and opened into a small meadow, which allowed Andria to ride up beside her. "Wayne shouldn'ta talked to you that way, Belle. It ain't right. And he sure shouldn't have hit you."

"I didn't exactly ask him to talk to me like that or to hit me, Andria. If you noticed, I ended up flat on my back."

"I noticed all right." Andria's voice was laced with anger. "The question is, what are we gonna do about it?"

"*We* aren't gonna do anything about it. For now we'll go into town like we were told. We'll let this die down a bit, and then I'll come up with a plan. Wayne'll expect somethin' from us now, so we'll wait till we can catch him off guard. When the time is right, we'll put my plan into motion."

two

Duncan slowed his horse as he rounded the last bend in the trail. He tilted his head and listened for the voices he thought he'd heard a few moments earlier. He'd diverted from the main trail—taking to a side path so he could water his horse—but the unexpected sounds in the brush up ahead caused him to slow his progress. Duncan knew enough from past experience to use caution when catching people unaware, especially out here on the less-frequented trails.

Sure enough, the rustle of fabric and the sound of harsh feminine laughter drifted his way on the breeze. They weren't the usual noises one would expect to hear while riding the trail, but they weren't completely uncommon either. Erring on the side of caution, he slipped his rifle from its place at the side of his saddle and rested it atop his legs as he quietly urged his horse to move forward. The laughter sounded again. It sounded anything but menacing, more self-deprecating, but Duncan wasn't taking any chances. The voices grew louder as he slowly rode closer.

"I wish you could see how funny you look." The speaker sounded young, her voice full of barely contained laughter.

"I'm glad you find this amusin'," a second voice chimed in, this one sounding older, less patient, and a bit more serious. "It's not like you don't have to follow suit. Whoever invented women's clothin' must have done so as a method of torture for someone they loathed."

Interesting. A woman complaining about wearing women's

11

clothing? That was something Duncan hadn't heard before. The situation grew more intriguing by the moment.

Duncan reined his horse to a stop as the first female laughed out loud. He didn't exactly want to ride up and surprise whoever appeared to be in the process of changing clothes on the other side of the trees. If he had the choice of another watering hole before heading back to town, he'd turn around and head in that direction. But since turning around wasn't an option considering the narrowness of the trail behind him, he figured he'd bide his time until they were finished, then he'd water his horse and move along when he could. It wasn't like he was hard-pressed to be anywhere specific at the moment anyway.

"Argh." More rustling of bushes as the more serious speaker shifted around. "I give up! Let's stay as we are, find a place closer to our destination where we can settle in for the night, and then we can change into these ridiculous clothes right before we walk into town tomorrow mornin'."

"Fine by me. You know I'm not happy about wearin' that awful dress in the first place. The less time I have to suffer through the experience, the better. I still don't see why Wayne wants us to wear the horrid things. He's only our brother. Why should we listen to him? Especially after what he did to you this mornin'."

"We'll do it because he told us to, Andria. I don't want you hurt. You know what he said; he wants us to blend in and not look like we just rode down the mountain. It's best for now that we do as he says. You have to stop fightin' the way things are, at least for now. Don't try to fight my battle for me."

Did they mean "hurt" physically? Or are they just talking about hurt feelings from an older brother's overprotective attitude? Duncan sure hoped it was the latter.

"Blend in?" the younger voice stated. "In these hideous things? How do you plan to do that?"

"We need to wear the dresses, Andria. We need Wayne to think we're in agreement with him. Our future plans depend on it."

From what Duncan could hear, these two couldn't "blend in" no matter how hard they tried. They were obviously from the hills, and judging from their conversation, they didn't often wear women's clothing. Their brother most likely wanted them to dress like ladies before their courting days began. Duncan smiled. He could only imagine what a handful two sisters like this would be for an older brother. Though he was curious to know what this older brother had done to his sister earlier in the day.

Duncan wanted to wait until they were dressed and then ride around the bend and introduce himself, but he was sure the women who were making the outrageous comments wouldn't appreciate his appearance. He'd wondered at times about the ridiculous outfits some women insisted on putting together, but he'd never considered that there were womenfolk who felt the same way—not that he thought about it often. As far as he knew, it was their lot in life to dress as they did, and none of them ever considered doing anything different.

These anonymous speakers taught him otherwise. Instead of approaching them, he figured he should find a way to turn around and head back along the trail that meandered through the trees. Perhaps if he could back the horse up a few feet, he could find a wider area and make his turn.

Instead of leaving, though, something compelled him to remain where he was. He heard more rustling, a few frustrated grunts, then two matching sighs of relief.

"Much better!" the older voice exclaimed. He heard the soft whinny of a horse. "I know one thing for sure. I completely prefer to wear pants over dresses. How do women get anything done in those things?"

"I dunno."

"Seems they'd be trippin' over their own skirts all the time. I certainly would be."

"Bella, about what you said—I'm not 'fightin'' things," the younger woman stated, her voice taking a hard edge. "I want to be more involved. I want more responsibility. Our brothers use us to do their biddin', yet they show us no respect. They'll learn to respect me before all is said and done." She paused. "And you'd do well to make them respect you as well."

Duncan leaned forward on his saddle. A warning sounded in his head. If these two women were in danger, he needed to intervene and at least offer up his help.

Bella didn't comment for a few moments, but when she did, her voice was tinged with resentment. "They'll never respect us, Andi. You'd do well to accept and understand *that*. What our brothers do—it ain't right. One of these days their actions will catch up with them, and I for one intend to be far away when that day comes."

"And how do you plan to get away? You have no money. The only time they let us out of their sight is to go up to Momma's place or when they come down here to a nearby town. This is the first time they've allowed us to come to town alone, and we have a tight timeline to work with. Without money, how do you ever plan to escape?"

Duncan hung back, wondering who Wayne was and why he treated his sisters so poorly. As the local parson, he wanted to help these hurting ladies. But he didn't want to burst in on their private moment. He assumed they wouldn't be receptive of his offer to help. As it was, he shouldn't have been eavesdropping on their conversation for as long as he had been. Maybe he could talk to the sheriff and together they'd be able to figure out a solution to provide for the women's safety.

He whispered a quick prayer for direction and was disappointed when he didn't feel led to interrupt their private discussion. God was clarifying what Duncan already knew. He needed to leave them alone for now.

The two women would head into town the next morning. He'd watch for them and have a plan in place when they arrived. For now, he needed to be on his way. They'd reach the trail at any moment, and he didn't want to be caught listening in. He looked around and noticed another, smaller trail forking off at an angle from the way he'd come. He decided to take the trail and see if it led to another watering hole farther downstream. In the meantime, he'd continue to pray for the women. He could still hear their voices as he backed his horse to the mouth of the smaller trail and moved away.

"Andria, I'll figure somethin' out. Just be patient and wait until I have a solid plan. We won't be under our brothers' control much longer."

"Well, I plan to be *in* control before much longer."

The voices still carried through the trees at his new angle. Duncan stopped again.

"Andria, don't say that! You'll only be hurt. There's no way our brothers will ever take orders from a mere *woman*. No one will ever force our brothers to change their ways. They're dangerous. Please promise me you'll listen and you'll wait for my lead before doing anything reckless."

Duncan debated going back. If he offered his help, maybe

he could provide a way for the two women to get away from their seemingly unstable brothers.

"What if I have a plan laid out before you come up with one?" Cockiness oozed through Andria's words.

"A plan to break away from the boys?"

"Maybe."

"Tell me before you act on it. We have a better chance of gettin' away if we work together."

"I'll tell you when the time is right."

"Andria—"

Duncan heard the younger woman's laugh as she urged her horse into action and burst through the trees behind him. He couldn't turn around on the narrow path but looked over his shoulder to see if he could identify the rider. He missed the first rider but saw a brief flash of auburn hair as the second rider gave chase. If he hadn't heard their feminine voices, he'd have been sure the riders were male based on their attire. He followed the new path until it opened up in a small clearing alongside the stream. He led Blaze toward the watering hole and offered up a prayer of thanks for God's provision, then added a petition for the safety of the two women he'd overheard.

After he'd watered his horse, Duncan followed the overgrown path to its end where it intersected with his original trail a good ways down the mountain from where he'd diverted to head for the water. He smiled, happy to know of another, quicker way to get through the area. He studied the mouth of the path that had all but disappeared once he'd cleared it. The surrounding landmarks would remind him of the path's presence in the future. Duncan's early days as an outlaw had taught him to watch for alternate trails. Back in his wilder days, he'd never known when he'd need a secondary escape plan. It was always best to have an alternate plan in place.

The old habit died hard and suited the life of a preacher just as well as it did a hardened outlaw. He glanced forward and noticed another rider approaching from the direction of town.

Duncan greeted the familiar man. "Afternoon, Jack."

"Howdy." Jack pulled his hat from his head and wiped his brow. The sun beat down hot on Duncan's back now that he had moved away from the trees. "Sheriff's looking for you, Duncan. I told him I'd pass the word along if I saw you on my way out."

"I appreciate it, Jack. I'm heading that way now. Anything serious?"

"Naw." Amusement passed through Jack's eyes. "I think he needs you to talk to a young prisoner."

"Ethan in trouble again?"

"Something like that." Jack put his hat back in place and firmed his grip on the reins, preparing to ride on. "He seemed pretty distraught."

"Ethan or his father?" The sheriff had his hands full with his young, errant son.

"Both."

"I can imagine. It's kind of hard for the sheriff to uphold the law when his own son thrives on breaking it."

"And it's hard for the boy to figure out how to spread his wings when his father's bent on clipping them."

"That's very true." Duncan's focus was on the unruly boy he'd grown so fond of when two riders flew around the bend of the main trail and startled both Jack's and Duncan's horses. The men fought to retain control of the scared beasts as the approaching riders skidded to a stop, fighting their own mounts as they reared backward.

"I'm so sorry," the farthest rider gasped. "We were in a hurry and didn't think about the fact that someone might be sittin' on the trail ahead of us."

Duncan recognized the voice and bright auburn hair. Bella. The nearer woman, the one Duncan guessed to be Andria, scowled.

As usual, God's providence caught Duncan by surprise. Even now, after all his training as a pastor, he was often awed by God's unfolding plans. He didn't know where this particular plan would lead, but he did know the shortcut had allowed Duncan to bypass the women when they'd taken the more visible upper trail.

He exchanged a curious look with Jack and shrugged. "No apology necessary. You're right. No one would expect to come upon someone sitting on the trail like we were. This isn't the place to be having a conversation."

"No harm done." The woman's smile was tight. She didn't allow time for introductions. "Come along, Andi."

Andria continued to scowl as they rode past.

"I'm—" Jack held up a hand but let his words die out as the women picked up their pace and hurried on down the trail. "Interesting pair."

Duncan watched them go. Even though he'd seen them face-to-face, he didn't know that he'd be able to identify them in town. They wore their hair pulled back in braids, and their faces were dusty from the trail. Their hats were pulled low on their foreheads. Intriguingly, they looked very much like two women who had a lot to hide.

three

Bella McLeod rode into a small clearing and motioned for her younger sister to stop. She figured this was as good a place as any to set up camp for the night. A bubbling brook beckoned from the other side of the trees, and the greenery and scrub formed a protective canopy over their heads. The cozy area lured her in, promising a peaceful experience that Bella often dreamed about but never quite achieved. Not with her brothers around, anyway.

"We'll stop here. In the mornin' we'll get up early, dress proper-like, and walk the rest of the way into town."

"You want to walk?" Andria shrugged and dismounted. "I s'pose that'll work. I still don't understand why we can't just ride the rest of the way in tonight, dressed as we are. We'd have an extra night to enjoy the sights before we take care of business. As a matter of fact, it would be the *perfect* time to take care of business."

"You mean you'd have an extra night to get into trouble." Bella shook her head. "I hardly think that's a good idea. You heard Wayne. He wants us to go in lookin' presentable, go about our business, and get out. He doesn't want us drawin' attention to ourselves by hangin' out in the saloon."

"You don't think we'll draw attention tryin' to look all ladylike when we're used to wearing men's pants and ridin' around on horses?" Andria challenged. "I'll probably trip on my skirt and fall flat on my face, just as you said before. And I'll likely take you down with me."

"You'll do no such thing. Don't talk like that. If you're focused on fallin' and get yourself all worked up about it, you'll fall sure enough."

"But people relax more in the evenin'. They let their guard down. I might be able to loosen a tongue or two over at the saloon and find out when the next posse'll ride out our way. Why waste a whole day eavesdroppin' around town when a simple question asked at the right time in the right place will do the job as well?"

Bella swung her leg over her horse and dropped down beside her sister. She busied herself with pulling items she'd need from the saddlebags that were slung over Steadfast's back. "The saloon is forbidden, Andi. You'll not step foot inside that place. We'll do as Wayne said, and we'll go about our business with our ears open. Nothin' more. Promise me you'll stick to the plan. I can't have you causin' trouble."

Andria stared at Bella, her expression calculating. Bella raised her eyebrows and stared back, daring Andria to challenge her. Her sister was fast gaining the reputation of a rebel, and Bella didn't like it.

"Andria, please. I want to keep you safe, and I can't do that if you run off and get into trouble."

"I can handle myself." Andria's eyes sparkled, and at the moment, Bella saw a little too much of Wayne in her younger sister.

Andria had something on her mind, and Bella wasn't sure she'd like it.

"Belle—I think I have a way to fix things."

"I'm sure you can handle yourself, but we need to do this together. We need to work as a team. We'll fix things *together*." Bella sighed, wondering how much she should share with her sister. "The boys are dabblin' in things they shouldn't be—"

"Nothin' new there. They've always dabbled in all the wrong things. It's not like I don't already know that."

"Maybe not, but they're changin' for the worse. Wayne's drinkin' more and actin' stranger than ever, and Charlie's bent on staying on his heels. Somethin' ain't right, and I don't like it. Until I know what's going on, we need to be careful."

"All right." Andria took up both horses' reins and led them toward the trees. The sound of running water bubbled from somewhere in the near distance. She stopped at the edge of the trees and glanced back. "You better promise me you'll tell me what's going on as soon as you figure it out."

"I promise." Bella smiled in relief and nodded. Her sister might be getting a stubborn attitude, but when she gave her word, she kept it. "You'll be the first to know."

Andria hesitated at the edge of the clearing, as if she wasn't completely sure she wanted to play whatever card she held. After a moment she blurted, "Bella, there's somethin' I need to tell you. Something that's gonna help us out." Her eyes sparkled with anticipation.

"Tell me now." Bella placed the items she'd been gathering on a nearby tree trunk.

Andria looked around. "Not here. Back by the water where no one can overhear."

Bella sighed. What was Andria up to? Her younger sister, the youngest of the McLeod clan, always seemed to get herself into fixes, but she never sounded as serious about any of the past offenses as she did about this.

They led the horses to the bubbling brook, a place Bella would find magical if she wasn't so worried about Andria's upcoming confession. The large oak trees closed in behind them to form a private oasis. Spanish moss drifted over the oaks' strong limbs. Birds serenaded from the treetops. Bella wondered what other secrets had been whispered under the protective branches of the trees.

The shallow stream to the right of them rushed over rounded rocks, each one polished smooth by years of tumbling water. The scent of jasmine filled the air. The water beckoned Bella, urging her to slip in and soak away the dirt and grime from the trail. Instead, she turned her focus on her sister.

"What have you done?" Bella knew she sounded judgmental, but years of experience led her to constantly question her sister's actions.

"I didn't *do* anythin'. I found somethin'. Somethin' wonderful." Excitement, fear, and wonder chased across Andria's features.

Bella frowned. "What did you find?"

"A treasure, Bella. Lots of it." She hesitated and licked her lips. "Bella—you and me—we're rich."

"Rich?" Confused, Bella studied her sister. She didn't seem to be teasing. But she doubted her sister knew what "rich" was. "How do you figure?"

"I was ridin' around up by the caves a few weeks ago—"

"The caves?" Bella shrieked. "You know you aren't allowed up there! It's dangerous. Wayne has repeatedly told us both to steer clear, unless the boys needed us and were nearby to offer protection."

No doubt about it, Bella needed to keep better track of her wayward younger sister. But Bella had her own responsibilities to tend to, which made it hard to keep track of Andria. Bella kept busy, and Andria was wily.

"Wayne needed me, Bella. I was on my way back home—"

"Wayne asked you to help with somethin' but didn't bother to ask me? Where was I?" Bella didn't like the implication of this. She'd talked to Wayne about making some changes a few times of late and had broached the topic of pulling out of the "family trade" and moving into something more reputable, but Wayne had laughed in her face.

She'd begged him, even suggesting doing something a bit more reputable like running moonshine, but Wayne would hear nothing of it. And now he'd cut Bella out of a situation and had used Andria by herself instead? Bella had a feeling she'd underestimated the depth of Wayne's anger.

"When was this?"

"It was when you went to gather Ma's dresses for this trip to town."

Wayne had sent Bella to their other cabin—Momma's place—while he used Andria to do his bidding. This couldn't be good. Bella had a really bad feeling about the whole situation.

"Andria, we need to get out. I don't like that Wayne's separatin' us. Next time he suggests this, I want you to tell me right away." Bella didn't want to think about what could have happened to Andi. "What did you find?"

"Gold and lots of it. It was hidden way back in one of the smaller caves. One we've never gone in before."

"The one I've told you to stay out of because of its instability?"

Andria had the grace to blush. "Yes. But nothin' happened. As you can see, I came out just fine." She motioned toward her intact body.

"But something could have happened and we'd have never known where you were. You can't just run off and do things like this, Andria. You mustn't be so impulsive."

Andria's expression changed to one of rebellion when she saw the flash of Bella's anger. Bella tamped down her frustration and changed her tone. "Okay, what's done is done, tell me more about the treasure."

"I went deep into the cavern, deeper than we've gone into the other caverns. . . ." Her voice drifted off as she watched for Bella's reaction.

Bella bit her tongue and fought to keep her lecture at bay.

"I had to light a lantern—it was really dark that far in. I'd decided to turn around and go back to the opening when I found these bags, they were just sittin' there against a wall."

She glanced over at Bella, and Bella nodded for her to continue.

"At that point I got scared. I realized someone else had been there, and whoever it was could either still be there or could come back at any time. Then I saw a skeleton. It scared me to death."

"So you decided to do the smart thing and get out of there?" Bella couldn't resist asking.

"Yes, as soon as I'd seen what was in the bags."

Bella rolled her eyes. "And?"

"Each bag was full of gold, Bella. They weren't huge bags, but it was a lot of gold just the same."

The thumping in Bella's head increased. "This is important, Andria. Did you tell Wayne or anyone else about the gold?"

Andria's eyes flicked away and back. She bit her lip. "No, you're the only one in the family that I've told."

"Andi. . ."

"I don't recall tellin' anyone else. Wayne for sure doesn't know. He'd gone off the other direction after tellin' me to head on home."

Bella had a feeling that Andria wasn't telling the whole truth, but there were more important matters at hand.

"Where is the treasure now?"

"I left it where it was. I couldn't carry it on my own, but I did grab a few pieces so I could show them to you." Andria slipped her hand into her pants pocket and pulled it out again.

Bella leaned forward as Andria gently unfurled her fist. Several small chunks of gold rested on Andi's open palm. The shafts of sunlight filtering through the trees glinted off the gold, making Bella's eyes hurt.

"Wow, you weren't kiddin'. It's beautiful."

"What do we do next? You'll help me get it, right, Bella?" Andria closed her hand and slipped the nuggets back into her pocket. She reached out and placed her hand on Bella's upper arm. "We can use the money to start over far away from here. We can get away from the boys. We can be free to live as normal folk, rich ones at that."

"We can't rush into anythin'." Bella chose her words carefully. Her heart was jumping at the thought of moving on. The possibility the gold offered them for a fresh start was enticing indeed. "We don't know who the gold belongs to, and we could get in a lot of trouble if we're caught with it."

"We could get into a lot of trouble by being caught with our brothers, too. I thought you wanted out?"

She had a point. Bella sighed. "I do want out. I just don't want to work ourselves into a worse situation in the meantime."

"How can it get any worse? If anyone finds out what our brothers do up in the hills, we'll be arrested right along with them. We *know* some of what they do up there, Belle, but we don't know all of it. You said so yourself. If we know about them robbin' and stealin' from people who pass through, what *don't* they want us to know? Why are they always sendin' us off before they join us back at the homestead?"

Bella had wondered about that many times herself, but she hadn't been able to sort things out. She always had Andi to consider and didn't want to put either of them at risk. When the boys told them to hole up at Momma's cabin, they did just that. Many times she'd been tempted to double back and watch to see what the boys were up to, but she knew Andi would be right on her heels and Bella couldn't take the chance.

Already, Andria seemed too enthralled with the boys' actions. She hated being left out of the mix. Bella tried to fight her sister's attraction to the outlaw ways, but if Bella didn't get her out soon, she knew it was only a matter of time before Andi gave herself over to that way of life completely. This was the first time Andria had insinuated she wanted a fresh start.

"If we work together to start fresh, you promise you'll change your ways?"

"I don't want to be a part of what the boys do. I want to live right, but if we're going to stay in, I want to be in control."

If the gold allowed them the opportunity to start a new life, who was Bella to say no? Who knew how long the treasure had been there. Bella couldn't let this opportunity get away. She'd sneak over to the cave and take a look at the situation herself before deciding, but if the gold looked to have been there for a while, she was taking it and her sister and leaving the hills to make a new beginning. She'd take personal satisfaction in the fact that her brothers had ruthlessly robbed people at gunpoint for so many years while the true treasure rested in their own backyard.

Bella nodded. "You have a point. We need to take action

now. Let's do what we came to do and then after we're back home, we'll talk about it some more and finalize our plans."

"The boys will likely send us to Momma's cabin after we tell them whether or not a posse will be arriving soon." Andria's expression was calculating.

"Yes."

"We can finalize our plans up there."

Bella sighed with relief. "Yes, we can."

Relief flooded Andria's features, too. Bella felt herself soften inside. Maybe Andria's rebellion of late had been her way of dealing with the desire to get out of the gang, not a desire to get further in.

With that thought in mind, Bella determined to get her sister safely away from the gang before she got in any deeper.

The decision to wait bought them some time. Bella could do some checking around before they walked into an even worse situation than they were already in. Maybe while they were in town she'd be able to find out if there had been a recent robbery nearby—one that involved a lot of gold.

four

"The problem with trying to be somethin' you aren't"—Bella stated as she pulled the voluminous amount of blue flower-adorned white cotton fabric over her head for the second time in as many days—"is the huge possibility that you'll get caught out of sheer stupidity. I still can't figure out top from bottom in this thing! How hard can it be to put on a simple dress? Other women do it on a daily basis."

Andria's contagious giggle carried through her own layers of fabric and over to Bella. Her entire mood had lifted since she'd shared about the gold. "Apparently, when you aren't used to wearin' them, it can be very hard. I'm afraid I'm permanently lost in here. How *do* women do this every day? I'd surely suffocate myself at some point. As a matter of fact, I think that's a huge possibility right now. It's so hot in here!"

Bella shifted her dress and pushed her head in another direction. The effort was for naught. Another barricade. "I don't see hide nor hair of daylight. What about you?"

"No." Andria's laughter still flavored her words. "I'm afraid I'm stuck somewhere between the linin' and the actual dress. I've taken a wrong turn somewhere."

Bella found the comment funny. "There *aren't* any linings in these dresses, Andria."

"Oh."

Andria's huffs and puffs of effort carried on the wind. Or maybe it was Bella's younger sister's attempt to breathe while stuck in a mix of frothy pastel pink fabric that made her sound so breathless.

"Belle, if someone stumbles upon us while we're like this, we're in trouble. We can't shoot while we're all tangled up in this constrictin' fabric. We should have dressed one at a time while the other stood guard."

The comment jolted Bella and urged her to find the right outlet for her head. "Fine time to realize such a thing, Andi! Why didn't you think of that a few minutes earlier? But who'd have thought we'd have so much trouble getting into the confounded things? We're women. By our very nature we should be able to dress in feminine attire."

At least they'd chosen the private area beside the stream to dress. It was less likely someone would stumble upon them way back here. Though if someone noticed their horses where they'd left them, they'd still be in trouble.

"Somethin' must be wrong with us. We're defective."

"You think so, Andria?" Bella winced at the level of sarcasm in her tone and gentled her approach. "We've been raised by outlaw brothers, and we're used to doing their biddin'. We dress in men's clothes, and we shoot like men."

"Well, it doesn't help that the only things we know about being a woman come from reading the books Ma had lyin' around before she died."

"Ma did a good job of trainin' us before she passed away. She gave us a good start before the boys took over and messed everything up. At least she taught us to read." Bella felt the fabric give as she found the correct opening and her head cleared the neckline. "Yes! I've made it through one openin'. There's hope for us, Andria."

"Can you shoot a rifle in your current position?"

"No." A sigh slipped past Bella's lips. Her arms were still

lost in the innards of the fabric mess. "Not without reversing the process and startin' all over. I could slip the rest of the dress back up over my arms and shoot in my undergarments, though that hardly seems proper. And I think that would sort of mess up our plans to eavesdrop and spy in town."

"Well, the good thing about that situation is the poor soul on the receivin' end would be so startled by a half-dressed female pointing a weapon at him, he'd likely not have time to react. You'd have a clear shot." Andria panted. She almost tipped over as she tilted and hopped at an odd angle. She looked more like an Indian warrior dancing around a fire than a fair maiden dressing for a trip to town.

"Right." Bella snorted. "They wouldn't be a bit distracted by your crazy dancin' and antics. And our brothers would thank us for taking the clean shot and ruinin' our scoutin' opportunity in town."

"Hmmm." Andria's head popped through her neck hole, and she sent Bella a pompous grin. "Then we'd best get to it and find our armholes so we can shoot proper-like."

"Well, I for one, don't intend to shoot anyone, dressed or not. I want to sashay into town, do our business, and be on our way. We have some plannin' to do."

"Oh, in that case, we're almost there."

Bella laughed out loud. Andria's hair stuck out every which way. Half the collar on her dress was tucked inside the neckline of her garment. The dress was twisted a quarter of the way around. One sleeve hung down her front and the other down her back. Andria looked like she'd just fought a very large bear and had come out on the losing end.

"What?" Andria frowned. "Please tell me I don't have it on inside out?"

"That would be the least of your worries." Bella would help

her, but her own arms were still lost in the fabric. She twisted and turned it every which way. "I'm thinkin' someone sewed the armholes shut by accident. I don't think my dress has any."

"That's because they're tucked inside. Your dress *is* wrong side out. The sleeves are, anyway." Andria tugged and shifted her pink fabric. "This bodice is so tight my arms won't fit through the armholes. Bella, what if the dresses don't fit?"

"They'll fit. Ma was bigger than either of us." Bella looked over to see the early morning sun rising a bit too quickly in the sky. "Slip the dress off your shoulders and lower the bodice down a bit. If you do that, your arms should be able to find the sleeves and you can pull it back up with everything in the proper place."

Andria did as told and sent Bella a smug look.

"You wouldn't be so far ahead if I hadn't walked you through the process," Bella muttered.

"If we'd pulled the dresses on feetfirst, we wouldn't have had such problems."

"Now you tell me," Bella muttered. "Why didn't you figure that out fifteen minutes ago?"

Andria sashayed over and pulled Bella's sleeves out properly. Bella slipped her arms through the thin fabric. She exchanged a glance with Andria and smiled. She knew no one watching their latest debacle would ever believe the danger the two women presented to others in their regular, everyday life.

۶

Duncan walked into the stifling heat of the sheriff's office and tossed his hat on the nearby desk. He could hear the sheriff muttering as he clattered around in the small back room. Duncan decided to give his friend some time and talk to Ethan first. He'd speak to the boy's father in a bit.

He turned his attention to the lone prisoner in the cell.

"Hey there, son. Looks like you've run into some problems today."

"I ain't your son." The boy's eyes narrowed, but even in the shadowy interior of the building Duncan could see the telltale remainder of tears. Ethan's eyes were red and swollen, but whether the tears were from sorrow or anger remained to be seen.

Duncan raised his arms above his head and braced them on the cool steel bars that separated the prisoners' quarters from the office. He rested his head on his forearms and studied his friend's only son. The boy was small in stature for a ten-year-old. Between that and his father's reputation as a no-nonsense sheriff, Ethan had a hard time of it with the other kids in town.

"Rough day?"

"I've had better." The sullen boy refused to look at Duncan.

"What're you in for this time?"

Ethan's scowl deepened. "Stealin'."

"Again? How many times is that this month? Three? Four? What'd you steal?"

"A lousy piece of candy." The scowl turned to a glare. "It ain't like old man Crawford can't afford it."

"Stealing is stealing, Ethan. It doesn't make it right just because someone has the money to buy more."

Ethan raised and lowered a shoulder.

Duncan walked over and rifled through the stack of odds and ends that lay upon Sheriff Andrew's desk.

"These things yours?" he asked as he picked up a small rock and tossed it up and down on the palm of his hand. Two similar rocks remained on the desk.

"Yes."

"This is a nice one."

"Yep."

"Where'd you find it?"

"Over at Cooper's Creek."

Duncan caught the pebble and turned it on his hand.

"Well, they sure are fine specimens. I think I'll keep this one for myself." He tucked the rock into his pocket and turned to go.

"Hey! Give that back!"

Duncan turned the boy's way and feigned surprise. "But you have two others just like it! What's it matter if I take just this one?"

"It ain't yours to take. You can get your own if you want to walk over there. I spent the better part of a hot afternoon looking for those three rocks."

"But you have three. I'm leaving you two others. You can walk over and get more just as well as I can."

"That don't matter. . . . They're still mine fair and square." By now the boy was standing on the other side of the bars, fists clenched. Duncan was aware that Sheriff Andrew stood just out of Ethan's line of vision in the back room, listening to the exchange with interest.

"Aw, Ethan, it ain't like you can't go over and get more when you get out of here. Isn't that pretty much the same thing as your theory on taking candy from Mr. Crawford?"

Ethan narrowed his eyes before dropping heavily down on the bed. "I get what you're doin'. I ain't dumb."

Duncan walked back over to the cell. "Then you know how Mr. Crawford must have felt when you walked out of there with something that wasn't yours to take."

"I guess so."

"So what do you propose we do about this, son?" Andrew stepped out into the main room. "I'd like to have you on your way home in time for the noon meal. Your ma'll tan your hide if you're late, especially when she finds out why."

"You ain't gonna tell her, are you?" Ethan seemed more worried about his mother's reaction to the theft than he did about his sheriff father locking him up. It was obvious who carried the big stick in the family home.

Duncan cupped a hand over his mouth to hide his grin.

"I dunno. Guess it depends on how you choose to deal with this."

Ethan's eyebrows pulled together in thought as he contemplated his dilemma. "I can tell Mr. Crawford I'm sorry."

"That's a good start," the sheriff said. He didn't seem bent on giving Ethan any breaks in this situation.

"Um." Ethan was silent a few minutes longer. "I can offer to sweep his back room for him." He looked sheepish. "Or maybe he'd rather have me out front where he can see me. I can sweep his porch for a week."

"A month," Sheriff Andrew agreed.

"A *month*? I only took one piece, and I didn't even get to eat it!"

"Keep that in mind next time you have a hankerin' to do wrong." Andrew's eyes narrowed, his expression resembling his son's earlier glare. "One month. I think that'll go a long way in making things right."

"Aw, Pa!"

"And you'll pay for the piece of candy."

"But I didn't get to eat it! That ain't fair! I threw it in those bushes when I heard you comin' and Patch ate it."

"It isn't fair that Mr. Crawford paid for that candy and can't make his profit or recoup his money for it. I guess your dog owes you a thank-you for his treat."

Ethan's shoulders drooped.

Andrew unlocked the cell and motioned his son to clear out. "You head on over to apologize and offer your assistance, then you get on home to your ma. *Straight* home. I'll follow up with Mr. Crawford as soon as I finish talking with Duncan. Don't make me sorry I let you go."

"I won't, Pa." The boy skirted his father and hurried for the door.

Duncan stopped him with a touch to his shoulder. "I want to see you in church on Sunday, Ethan."

"Yessir." Ethan raced out the door.

As soon as it slammed shut, Andrew sank into his chair. "That one's going to do me in, Duncan. How am I supposed to keep the law when I can't even control my own son? I'm feeling the need to hang up my hat."

"You mean, hang up your hat as in turning in your badge? You'd quit as sheriff just because you have a rambunctious son?"

Andrew motioned Duncan into the seat opposite him. "It isn't just that. I'm feeling old and tired. I've lost my edge. I'm hearing new rumblings about the McLeod gang, and people are starting to talk. They want something done about them. I've been after that gang for years and haven't gotten anywhere when it comes to stopping their outlaw ways."

"The McLeod gang is good. Better men than us have tried and failed to capture them."

"I know, but they've become a personal thorn in my side, and I want to put them behind bars. If I can't, I need to find someone who can."

"So you're going to toss that desire to capture them aside and quit?"

Andrew slammed his hand down on his desk. "I didn't say

that. I said I *feel like* hanging up my hat, not that I am."

"Just asking some questions based on your comments, Andrew." Duncan raised his arms in mock surrender. His friend was strung tight today. "What do you plan to do?"

"I guess I'll put together a posse and ride up there. See what we can find out."

"A posse?" Duncan didn't like that idea. Several other posses had ridden up into the hills, only to have several come back injured. No one could prove the McLeods were responsible, but speculation leaned in that direction. "I'd rather you not do that. You know what's happened to the others."

"No, we *don't* know; that's part of the problem. We don't know who is behind the attacks. I'd like to find out." Andrew stood and paced the length of the small office.

"You have a wife and son to consider. Let's figure out another way."

"That's just the point. I do have a wife and son to consider. I'm not doing them any favors by sitting down here waiting for the McLeod gang to strike again."

Duncan studied his friend. "You know something." It wasn't a question.

Andrew stared out the window. After a few moments, he turned to look at Duncan. "You had lunch yet?"

"No."

"Let's head over to the diner, and I'll tell you what I know. I trust your intuition and will listen to your thoughts after I've shared."

"I'm ready to head over there now."

five

Duncan studied the street that ran through town as they walked to the diner. Other than wisps of road dust hanging in the air from the most recent traveler, the steaming stench of horse manure lingering in the midday heat, and the normal parade of people coming and going from the shops and eating establishments, he saw nothing out of the ordinary. He'd hoped to catch a glimpse of the two sisters when they rode into town, but so far he hadn't seen any sign of them. He supposed they could blend in from afar if they'd decided against the dresses and to instead wear the clothes from the day before.

He and Andrew chose a small table in the far back corner of the diner. The choice gave them privacy to talk while allowing the sheriff a clear view of the room and roadway outside the front windows.

Sheriff Andrew leaned forward, his face close to Duncan's. "Rumor has it that the youngest McLeod family member— Alex—has the missing gold from the big mine heist several years back. Do you remember that one?"

Duncan's blood ran cold as he nodded. He remembered all right. The heist occurred a year before Duncan became pastor of their small town.

"We need to gather another posse to chase the McLeods down and see what they know. We'll bring the youngest member in for questioning. Maybe that'll make the older ones talk, too."

"Don't count on it." Duncan tried to keep his voice steady. He'd turned his life over to Christ years ago and had kept steady in his relationship with Jesus ever since. This news put Duncan in a dilemma. The situation had the potential to collapse his carefully constructed life, but at the same time he couldn't let his tenuous situation cause innocent people pain.

"Don't count on finding them, or don't count on the older ones talking to protect a younger one?"

"Both." Duncan shifted on his chair. "You know their reputation. They're mean as snakes and as sneaky as ever. They won't care if you have one of their younger siblings."

"You're sure?" Andrew rested his chin on his hand, his expression thoughtful. "What do you recommend? Someone needs to go up there."

"Give me some time to think and pray about it." Duncan would do more than think. He'd figure out a plan that didn't involve the sheriff or a posse.

The door to the diner opened, and the room grew silent. Duncan and Andrew turned their attention to the newcomers. Two women stood in the doorway looking around the room with discomfort as every eye in the place stared them down.

Duncan had been wrong when he'd thought Bella and her sister could slip into town unnoticed. Cleaned up, they were two of the most beautiful women Duncan—and apparently most every man in the diner—had ever seen.

Several men jumped into motion at once. One even tipped his chair over in his hurry to get to the entry before the others. The two women stepped backward in alarm. They obviously hadn't foreseen or planned to create a stampede when they entered the establishment.

Madelyn Steeples, the diner's owner, bolted through the

kitchen doorway and bustled toward the newcomers. She waved her heavy arms in the air. "Shoosh now! You men go on back to your seats and sit yourselves down. Imagine getting all caught up in a frenzy just because two pretty ladies walk through our door." She hemmed and hawed as she hustled across the diner.

No one questioned Maddy when she was on a mission. Several men left, and the few remaining men hurried back to their seats and conversations as directed, but their eyes remained focused on the women. Maddy glanced around the room. Her search ended when she noticed Duncan and Andrew in the far corner. She motioned for the two women to follow her and led them to the table across from the men. The dark-haired woman stumbled, and the other steadied her with a hand to her arm.

"Sheriff? Parson? I assume you two can welcome these ladies into your conversation without causing a disturbance?"

"Of course we can." Duncan hurried to stand and pulled out a chair for the nearest woman, Bella, the one with the fiery-colored hair. Both sisters had vivid blue eyes. Andrew stood and pulled out a chair for the younger, dark-haired sister.

"Bella and Andria, right?"

Bella froze in place, gaping at him.

Duncan smiled. "I'm Duncan Bowers. We met on the trail yesterday afternoon. I heard you refer to each other by name. I was one of the men blocking the path when you rode down the trail."

Bella relaxed and settled into her seat. "I remember."

"Allow me to introduce the sheriff, Andrew Walker."

"It's a pleasure to meet you, Sheriff Walker." Duncan

noticed her discomfort. She looked anything but happy to meet him.

"Sheriff Andrew is fine."

"Sheriff Andrew, then."

Andrew didn't move. The women's expressions went from uncomfortable to panicked.

Duncan hurried to finish introductions. "I'm sorry. Sheriff, this is Andria and Bella. . . ?"

"Um. . ." Bella hesitated.

"McLeod," Andria supplied.

Bella flinched and stared forward, not meeting Duncan's or the sheriff's eyes.

McLeod? Providence. Yet again.

Duncan smiled. "Andria and Bella McLeod."

"Nice to meet you." To his credit, Andrew didn't bat an eye as the ladies identified themselves as possible relatives of the gang Duncan and Andrew had just been discussing moments earlier.

Maddy walked up and delivered Duncan's and Andrew's food. The savory scent of pot roast and baked vegetables— herb-topped potatoes, carrots, and onions—drifted up and teased Duncan's senses. Maddy placed a basket of yeasty-smelling bread and a small container of butter on the table between them before turning to take Bella's and Andria's order. Andrew tucked a napkin on his lap, and Duncan picked up his fork, ready to enjoy the succulent meal. As soon as the women were distracted with their menus, Andrew sent Duncan a pointed look, and Duncan nodded imperceptibly.

After Maddy moved off to the kitchen with their order, Andrew began his interrogation. His experience as sheriff showed as he mixed bites of food with well-targeted questions.

"So what brings you ladies to town? Do you have business here? Or do you have family in the area?"

This time Bella sent Andria a look and stepped into the position of spokeswoman. "A little bit of both. Our family lives up in the hills, but we came to town to order some supplies."

"I see." Andrew casually leaned back in his seat, folding and unfolding his napkin. "Will you be here for a few days, then?"

"No, we'll see to our business and be on our way in the mornin'."

Duncan watched as the sheriff leaned forward. He frowned. "I have to say I'm surprised and a bit nervous to see two women travelin' such a distance without a chaperone. As sheriff I know the risks of such a thing."

Bella exchanged a glance with Andria and smiled. "I appreciate the concern, Sheriff, but we can handle ourselves just fine."

"I'm sure you can, but it doesn't seem right for me to let y'all ride out in the mornin' without a proper escort."

Duncan had a feeling he wasn't going to like what Andrew was going to say next.

Bella apparently felt the same way. A hint of irritation passed over her features. "I can assure you, Sheriff Andrew, we're completely able to take care of ourselves. We've never had a problem travelin' alone before, and we've traveled the hills quite extensively."

"I'm glad to hear that, but all the same, you're here on my watch. I couldn't in good conscience let y'all leave here without proper protection." He smiled and motioned toward Duncan. "Duncan often acts as my deputy, in addition to his duties as the parson. He's completely trustworthy in both capacities. If Duncan is in agreement, I'd like to have him accompany you home."

Duncan cringed. He didn't feel comfortable with Andrew forcing his company on the women, but he felt even more uncomfortable with the sheriff's words of affirmation. The only thing he'd ever kept from the sheriff was that in his former life—before turning his life over to Christ—he, too, had lived as an outlaw. His past wasn't all that different from the McLeods'.

❧

Bella watched as Duncan's mouth gaped open. Bella felt hers do the same. They exchanged similar horrified glances. The only sound came from Maddy, who worked at the far end of the diner wiping down tables and carrying dirty dishes from the tables to the kitchen. The room grew uncomfortably quiet as the other diners trickled out the door to return to their afternoon obligations. Bella wished she and Andria were ready to do the same. But it wouldn't do to draw further attention by leaving before their meals arrived.

"I appreciate the consideration, but an escort is not necessary." Bella bit out her words through clenched teeth. She kept the smile pasted on her lips, but she knew the smile didn't reach her eyes. Instead she felt pure panic at the thought of this kind and peaceful man escorting them home. "We don't need a chaperone."

Wayne wouldn't be happy to have a man brought into their encampment, let alone a law-abiding one. Bella had no idea how she could warn or protect the parson without giving herself away. The sheriff didn't seem to recognize their family name when Andria blurted it out, but Wayne would be sure to cover their tracks when it came to a stranger approaching their territory. And she had no doubt that Wayne would find out.

"The trip is long and hard. We don't live close by. We couldn't possibly ask the parson to make such an arduous trip."

Duncan seemed to gather himself. He grinned at her statement. "I'm sure I'm up to the trip. I mean, you two seem to have made it here just fine. I'm sure I can make it up the mountain just as well."

Bella studied him. He wasn't the kind of pastor she was familiar with, not that she had a lot of experience in that area. The one who'd buried her father and mother had been a skinny, mean, beady-eyed old man who walked stooped over his cane. His eulogies, as far as she could recollect, at each of her parents' funerals were something to the effect of "good riddance." Her father had deserved such a send-off; her mother did not.

Bella knew that in most of her neighbors' eyes—not that the neighbors were that much better—her mother was guilty by association. It didn't matter that she came from back East and had an educated background. She'd married a scoundrel, which placed her in a similar category. The horrible old man who buried her momma made sure the few people at the funeral knew that, too.

Duncan, on the other hand, was the complete opposite of that other pastor. He was tall, strong, and ruggedly handsome. He wore his long dark hair pulled back at the neck, and he had compassionate brown eyes. Even in the midst of her horror at the thought of him accompanying them home, she could only imagine what it would be like to have someone like him watching out for her and Andria. She could think of far worse company to keep—her brother Wayne's for starters. The thought quickly reminded her of why she didn't want nor need the parson to ride along with them to their homestead.

"Actually, our older brother will be ridin' out to meet us. He won't take too kindly to us appearin' in the presence of a man he doesn't know." She hesitated. "Nothing personal or anythin', but he'd shoot first and ask questions later."

"I wouldn't do anything different if you were my sisters," Duncan observed.

"But you would have arranged for a proper escort for your sisters in the first place," Bella stated, her voice flat. The man didn't back down easily.

"I would have, yes." He nodded, his eyes warm. "And if they'd snuck off on their own, I'd have ridden out to find them."

He must think their brother a complete miscreant. Of course, if Duncan did think that, he'd be right.

"Well, you aren't our brother. And we didn't sneak off on our own. Our brother knew where we were going. He sent us here. He had business to attend to elsewhere. But I'll have you know he's very possessive—I mean, protective—in his own way."

"I can only imagine."

"Then you'll understand why you can't escort us home?"

"No." Duncan shook his head. "I'll still escort you. I'll just be on my best behavior, and I'll be ready when we meet up with your brother."

Bella sighed none too quietly. She started to say something else but decided against it. She'd just have to come up with a plan to dodge him. They would leave at daybreak. She'd make sure they were long gone before Duncan-the-parson ever had a chance to join up with them.

six

"*McLeod*, Andria?" Bella admonished the moment they'd finished their meal and cleared the doorway of the diner. "Why didn't you just hold up a sign that says SISTERS OF THE NOTORIOUS MCLEOD GANG?"

"Well, I didn't see that you were comin' up with anything better. You just sat there stutterin'—your eyes all big and startled-like—while you floundered around in your head for a last name that would work. Do you seriously think that looked any better than my just tellin' the truth? And we aren't just 'sisters' of the notorious McLeod gang, we're a *part* of it."

Bella walked in silence for a moment, considering Andria's words. "I, for one, prefer to be known as the McLeod clan."

"Prefer whatever you want, but the hard truth is, we're in this as deep as our brothers, reluctant participants or not."

"I don't want to be a part of it, Andria, and I don't want you to be, either. We've gotta get out."

"How we gonna do that with Deputy Parson on our heels? That'll be a fine mess when we lead him straight to the homestead. Wayne'll be beyond thrilled. Have you forgotten how he knocked you from that horse? He'll do far worse when we show up with the law."

"You don't think I know that, Andi? We've gotta come up with a plan." Bella had been deep in thought throughout their entire meal and still hadn't figured out the best way to handle things. If they slipped out early, they'd draw attention. The wrong kind of attention. But showing up at the homestead

46

with a man wasn't an option, either.

"Do you think he's onto us? Neither one of them seemed too familiar or surprised when I shared our last name."

"Can't tell with the likes of them. Sheriffs and preachers can be clever that way. I didn't see either one of them as bein' stupid." Bella ducked into the mercantile to place their order. She pulled out her short list and handed it over to the proprietor.

"Hello, ladies." The man's lecherous eyes surveyed them from top to bottom as he leaned forward with his elbow braced on top of the counter. "Ain't seen neither one of you around these parts before." He smirked. "And I would have remembered if I'd seen your pretty faces before."

"We're just passin' through." Bella's smile felt tight. "We have some other business here in town so we'll be on our way. Would it be possible for you to wrap our order and have it ready when we return?"

"I can do better than that." He glanced around and leaned closer. His yellow-toothed smile looked more predatory than friendly. "Tell me where y'all are stayin' for the night, and I can personally deliver your order right to your door."

"That won't be necessary." Bella slipped her small money pouch over her wrist.

The man eyed them suspiciously. "What's your business in town?"

Bella started to tell him to mind his own business, but Andria stilled her with a touch of her hand. Much to Bella's disgust, Andria batted her eyes at the despicable man and gave him a conspiratorial smile. "You seem like the kind of man who knows what's goin' on around town. Any word on the outlaw gang that's rumored to live up in the hills? Is it true they're robbin' and raidin' and that people are gettin' upset?"

"Why would two women like you care about some ole gang?"

Andria smiled, her eyes dreamy. "I just think it'd be so excitin' to meet up with the likes of someone like that."

Bella almost choked. Contrary to her sister's ruse, they wanted to be far away from the likes of Wayne and his outlawin' ways.

"Well, hon, you want a rebel-type man, you got someone like that right here in front of ya."

Bella's stomach turned. "We need to go—"

"Oh please, sis. I just gotta find out if the rumors are true." Andria returned her attention to the proprietor. "*Are* they?"

"They're true, all right. According to local gossip, the sheriff is forming a posse to go up into the mountains and force the whole mess of 'em out of the hills and into custody. He'll take 'em dead or alive."

Bella shivered. She could fully imagine Sheriff Walker uttering similar words during discussions on how to best capture the gang.

If what the proprietor said was true, it was likely the sheriff knew exactly who she and Andi were and that's why he'd suggested Duncan ride along. Duncan would be able to scout out the situation under the guise of accompanying the sisters on the trip home. And if Duncan found out they were indeed related to the McLeod gang, she and Andi would be arrested—or worse—right along with their brothers.

"We have to be goin' now." Bella pulled Andria by the arm when it appeared her sister wanted to pump the man for more information.

The proprietor slicked back his oily hair with his hand while leering at Andria with a grin. Bella frowned with disgust. He used the same hand to pick up the list of items Bella needed to take home, leaving a greasy oil spot on the previously pristine piece of paper. She scowled. "We'll be back top of the next hour."

"I'll be waitin'." His answer was directed toward Bella, but his gaze and innuendo were focused on Andria.

Bella hurried from the store. "No way does the sheriff not recognize our name, Andria."

"I was thinkin' the same thing." Andi frowned. "Question is, what are we gonna do about it? You still want to give that sheriff the slip? They could arrest us before we report to Wayne if we do."

Bella considered her words. "I don't think so. I think they would have arrested us already if they wanted us in custody. They want Wayne and Charlie."

"Or perhaps they want all of us together."

"That's possible, too."

They headed toward the far end of town. Bella was too riled up to stick around in any one place while they waited for their purchase to be gathered. She moved quickly down the walkway. She had a thought and whirled around, nearly knocking her sister over. "But then again, maybe they don't see us as outlaws. Maybe they assume we're innocent victims of our brothers' wild ways—which we are to a point."

Andria's eyes lit up. "And if they capture Wayne and Charlie, we'll be free to move on and start fresh."

Bella grinned. "That means our little farce is workin' out. The sheriff must see us as the innocent women we've been trying to portray."

They reached the end of the walkway and turned around.

Bella admitted something that was bothering her. "I hate to think of Charlie facin' the same future as Wayne. Charlie still cares. We might have a chance of reachin' him. What do you think?"

"You want to let him in on our plans?" Andria's face scrunched. "I'm not sure I trust him that much."

"No, I don't trust him, either. I think his loyalties run toward Wayne. As much as I love him, I think he's closer to becomin' like Wayne than wantin' to be like us."

"He did take up for you when Wayne knocked you from the horse. You have to remember that."

Bella reached back and touched the knot that had formed at the back of her head after Wayne had knocked her down. She knew she had a large bruise on her shoulder, considering the raw tenderness she'd felt when she'd tried to lie on her back the night before. "He did. But then his only counsel was for me to be more careful around Wayne. He didn't say anythin' that would give me the idea that he was tired of the way Wayne treats us."

"You have a point." Andria folded her arms. "What do you think will become of them if the posse locates the other homestead? If anything happens to the boys, we'll be completely on our own."

"We've pretty much been on our own since Momma died, Andi. Losin' our brothers won't change things much."

"True." Andria shrugged. "In that case, I guess things would change for the better. I don't want to wish ill on them—I want them to change and do better things with their lives—but if they weren't around, we could stay on at Momma's place, fix it up, and continue our lives here. I could resume my friendship with Sarah, and it would be like old times."

Andria had a point. The boys had made their lives miserable, so why should she and Andria be the ones to leave? If they could get their brothers to go out West without them, they'd be able to set up a new life of their own. "But what if they leave for a while and then return? We'd always have that concern to worry about."

"Then we need to continue with our plans to leave and hope that the boys make it through whatever they end up facin'."

Bella nodded. She didn't want to think about her brothers' fate. At the moment, their fate was too intertwined with her own. And with Andi's. Whatever happened to Wayne, Charlie, and herself, she had to make sure Andi escaped and had the chance to live a life free of their outlaw ways. She was so young. She didn't have many memories of their life as a family. She deserved a chance to be happy and to find a family to settle down with.

But Bella was concerned that if Andria alone made it through whatever came their way in the future, Andria'd be so angry she'd never settle for a normal life. Instead, Bella figured Andi would gravitate toward the saloons and meet up with someone there and her life wouldn't be any better than it was at the present.

Bella felt there had to be something more out there. Something good. After all this was over and they were free, she'd find a parson and talk things over with him. Duncan came to mind. He intrigued her as much as he annoyed her. She'd love to spend more time in his company if things were different.

Bella stood at the end of the walkway and surveyed the street that ran through the mountain valley. Earlier that morning, when they were on their way in, Bella hadn't taken the time to see the small town's charm. Nestled in the foothills of the mountains, the town had looked smaller than it really was. It boasted a good-sized bank and two mercantiles. If Bella had noticed that fact before, she'd have left the one they'd patronized and would have gone on to do her business with the other one. She continued her perusal. The town also had a milliner, the diner, and a dress shop. A good-sized livery finished out the far end of the strip on the opposite side of the road.

Their side of the street held two saloons, a boardinghouse, the general store where they'd placed their order, and at the far end, the sheriff's office.

People bustled in and out of the various establishments, going about their day. No one paid Bella or Andria any mind as they stood forlornly at the end of the road. Bella tried to imagine living in a place like this, a place where neighbors called each other by name and waved to one another with friendly familiarity, a place where others were there to look out for you when you were ill or were facing hard times.

Bella shook herself out of her musings and glanced back toward the diner. Duncan and Andrew stood just outside the door of the establishment, deep in conversation. Duncan glanced her way and grinned. He sent her a small wave, and the sheriff looked over. Bella felt her face flush with guilt, though in theory—or at least as far as they knew—she'd done nothing wrong. She walked over to the wooden rail that separated the walkway from the road and leaned her elbows against it. If she couldn't even stand in the same town with Duncan without blushing and feeling guilty about her family's outlawin' ways, how would she ever travel all the way home with him by her side?

On the other hand, she had so many questions about life and how things worked out in the normal world, she would enjoy having a few moments alone with the parson. Maybe he could help her know how to live a different life. If she had a chance, she'd ask him about God and what He thought of people like her. She'd ask him how she could help her sister find more to life than the hand they'd been dealt so far. Maybe he could intervene in Andi's life and help her find a better way. Bella longed for a better way, but she didn't feel she deserved it.

It wasn't like she didn't know what her brothers did. They stole from people on the trails—robbed unsuspecting travelers—and left them stranded far from town. And as she and Andi had discussed the previous day, Bella had her suspicions that Wayne's outlaw ways had reached new levels in recent months.

Something deep inside Bella warned that he'd escalated to harsher crimes and that she and Andi needed to get away. The feeling had intensified when she'd been in the presence of Parson Duncan. She felt he held the reins to her future, but unfortunately—for his safety and their own—she and Andi would have to head out long before he had a chance to hand them over.

seven

Bella looked like a lost lamb. More than likely, based on her family history, she was a lost lamb—at least in the eyes of God. Duncan parted ways with Andrew and wandered over to lean against a nearby wall. He took the opportunity to study her. A few moments earlier when he and Andrew had exited the diner, Andria and Bella had been in deep conversation. Now Bella rested against the rail in front of her, looking as if she carried the weight of the world on her shoulders. Andria paced back and forth behind her, looking bored. After a few more turns, she glanced around and headed down the walkway. She kept her eyes focused downward as she approached.

When she walked by, she tossed her black curls over her shoulder and sent him a saucy grin. She didn't stick around long enough to offer a chance for conversation, which was fine with Duncan. If he spoke with anyone, he wanted it to be Bella. Duncan nodded his head at Andria, looked back at Bella, and decided he'd take advantage of this opportunity and talk with her while she was alone. He knew she wasn't happy about their upcoming trip, and he felt he should try to alleviate any concerns she might have about the travel arrangements. Maybe if they could talk a bit, she'd be more open to his company.

Bella didn't react to his approach. Either she was really good at ignoring people she didn't want to talk to, or she was so caught up in her thoughts that she hadn't heard him walk up behind her. He suspected the latter. And if it was the latter, he had all the more reason to accompany them home. It wasn't a good idea to be unaware of your surroundings when traveling away from home. Like Andrew, Duncan wouldn't rest until he knew Bella and Andria were safely back at their place in the hills.

Duncan cleared his throat to announce his presence. "I guess you've already finished your shopping?"

Bella jerked upright and spun around. Even at full height she was still a good six inches shorter than his six-foot-tall stature. He towered over her. In an instant her expression changed from contemplative and wistful to challenging and hard. She glared up at him.

"I've placed my order, yes, and I'm waitin' for it to be filled." Her tone was defensive. "We'll head out as soon as it's ready."

"Head out, as in going home? Or head out, as in leaving town and staying put until morning?"

She blatantly ignored the question.

He took her place at the rail, hoping the casual action would put her at ease. She held her position, standing rigidly behind him and slightly to his right. He waited to see if she'd answer. Most women hated silence and would fill in any awkward moment with lame conversation. Since the silence didn't seem to bother her, Bella obviously wasn't one of them.

Duncan watched as a horse and wagon came into sight from around the farthest building to the south of town. A young family sat upon the front bench, smiling and talking as they rolled past. Duncan wondered if he'd ever have such an experience. He kind of hoped so. The family seemed so content.

He decided to break the silence. "Thomas Mercantile or Sundry's Dry Goods?"

"Pardon?" Bella stepped closer, her forehead crinkled with confusion.

"We have two stores in town. Which shop did you place your order with?" He looked over at her. She looked like she'd rather be anywhere else but there.

"Oh—" She leaned around him and glanced down the road toward the two shops and read the closest sign. "Thomas Mercantile, I guess."

"Sundry's might be a better choice next time—that is, if you ever plan to come back down this way. Thomas can be a bit much to deal with, especially when pretty women enter his shop alone."

"So I noticed." Bella flushed. "But I didn't know before we went in. I'll keep that in mind for the future. Thank you."

"My pleasure. I'm here to help the townspeople—or those like you in the surrounding areas—in any way I can." He sent her a grin that she didn't respond to. He felt his smile falter. "Anything a person might need or might want to talk about—spiritual guidance, advice on situations that occur in day-to-day living, safety issues that might cause concern. . .all you have to do is ask."

She flinched. He wished he could ask outright about the conversation he'd overheard the previous day, but he couldn't.

"I'm not much for askin'." She stood close beside him but kept her gaze on the building across the street. She hugged herself tight, her arms wrapped defensively around her chest.

"So I've noticed." He chuckled.

Her brilliant blue eyes narrowed as she turned to stare into his. As he watched, a few tendrils of her gold-tinged hair fell forward to frame her face. The slightly curled tresses cupped her cheeks and softened her features. "Are you laughin' at me?"

"No!" He straightened, his arms raised in a gesture of innocence. "Of course not. Never."

"Then why did you laugh?"

"I wouldn't exactly call that a laugh."

"What *would* you call it?"

He thought a moment. "I guess if I had to call it anything, it would be a chuckle."

"Why did you *chuckle* at me?"

He sighed in exasperation. "I didn't laugh or chuckle at you! I found your words to be amusing. You leave no doubt that you're perfectly capable when it comes to your ability to take care of yourself or to find your way on your own. Based on that, I figured you for the type to resist asking for help, even if you needed it."

"Oh. Capable." Her tough facade cracked a bit, and she scowled. "I wouldn't go that far."

Duncan knew enough to proceed with caution now that he'd found a chink in her armor. He remained silent, letting her take the lead.

She didn't elaborate further.

"You have doubts about your capabilities, Bella?"

"I have doubts about pretty much everything. Doesn't everyone?"

"I'm sure they do." He was pleased with himself. This was the longest conversation he'd had with her since they'd met. Their conversation at the diner was forced, with her mostly answering their questions in as few words as possible. A warm breeze blew past and rustled the leaves on a nearby magnolia, distracting him. He figured Bella would look pretty with one of the tree's white blossoms tucked into her hair.

"What are yours?"

Distracted by the direction of his musings, he lost his train of thought. "My what?"

"What are your doubts?"

The question caught Duncan off guard. He was used to being in control of conversations. Bella seemed to have a way of keeping him off balance. He was used to doing the asking and getting answers from everyone else. No one came to see the parson to ask about his life or to see to his needs. They came to him when they needed something from him, which was exactly what he expected.

Of course the women in town took good care of him, dropping by regularly to stock his pantry or to drop off a baked good or two in appreciation of some service he'd rendered. The men in his congregation came around now and then to drop off a stack of firewood for the parsonage or to fix something on the church grounds. The single women kept his dinner table well stocked when he was in town, which was part of the reason he liked to roam around the hills as much as he did during his off days. The townspeople took good care of him, but they never asked questions about his well-being. They never asked about his personal thoughts or feelings.

That is, no one had until now.

Duncan suddenly found himself on the receiving end of questions he wasn't sure he wanted to answer. Questions he didn't want to think about. He figured for a man in his position, he doubted far too much as it was. And he wasn't sure he wanted to admit that. He knew better. He studied the Word. But still he found himself questioning God in various areas. Not all the time, but far too often. Like when someone in his small church passed away unexpectedly and he had to help the family with their grief. Or when a family worked hard to bring in a crop and too much rain or not enough moisture took everything they had. And on the other hand, he found himself surprised when God acted in ways that caught him off guard, but he figured he shouldn't be surprised at God's provision at all. He was still a work in progress. "I'm not sure how to answer that."

Bella's mouth turned up at the corner. The smile radiated through to her eyes. She had a beautiful countenance. "So the preacher doesn't like to admit his shortcomin's? Or does your strong faith allow you to cast aside all your doubts? Perhaps you don't ever have any?"

"I wish I could say that." He smiled. As pastor, Duncan wanted to reach out and use this small connection they'd forged as a way to get to know Bella better. He also wanted to be sure to represent himself in a way that was honest and reflected where he was on his faith journey. But he didn't want to be a stumbling block to someone who was obviously searching. "I'm sure I'm no different than you, Bella, or anyone else in this town. I often struggle with doubt. Faith is an ongoing process; trust isn't something that happens overnight."

"But you're a pastor."

"That doesn't make me perfect."

"Hmm." Her forehead wrinkled, and she nibbled on her lower lip. "That's an interestin' way to put it."

"Why?"

"I just always thought preachers had faith, and that was that. I didn't figure they struggled with the same things us common folks struggle with."

"I have complete faith in my Lord Jesus Christ and His ability to do what's best for me. But like anyone else, I tend to let my doubts about how things are going to work out creep in now and again." He turned to face her. "Everyone struggles, Bella. Pastors, believers, nonbelievers. The difference is that faith helps a believer get beyond the struggle and on to the other side."

"Believers? Nonbelievers? I'm afraid I have no idea what you're talkin' about."

"Believers are those who turn their lives over to Christ. They want to live a life that's pleasing to Him. They're followers of Jesus. They turn to the Bible for advice on how to live their life, and they want to do good."

"So you're sayin' if I'm a nonbeliever, I have no hope of comin' through a struggle on my own?" She frowned, her frustration evident.

"No, I'm not saying that at all. You can come through your struggles just fine, but you're going it alone. We all sin—we all do bad things or have moments where we choose to do wrong in our lives. A relationship with Jesus means you don't have to go it alone. Jesus forgives those sins. All a person has to do is ask. Faith brings peace and gives hope. That doesn't mean the hard times go away; they're just easier to handle when they do come."

"So you're sayin' as a nonbeliever, I have no hope?" Bella looked as lost as she sounded. Her hands rubbed up and down her arms as if she were cold.

Duncan's heart went out to her. He softened his voice. "I'm saying with Jesus there is all hope."

❧

Bella wanted hope. She also wanted peace. Her thoughts were in constant turmoil. The constant unrest in the life she lived exhausted her. She wanted to know and understand the deep faith that shone from Duncan's brown eyes. His eyes were kind and compassionate in a way she'd never seen before, and she had a hard time looking away from them.

In fact, she had a hard time looking away from his face in general. Everything about him was pleasing to the eyes. Gold streaks wound through his wavy brown hair and spoke of a man who spent a lot of time outdoors. His jaw was strong and his lips—well, she had the silliest urge to lean in and see what they would feel like against her own. Never in all her life had she ever given consideration to such a thing! Her emotions were making her crazy.

Duncan was kind in nature, too. His strong physique hid a gentle spirit. No man had ever taken the time to talk with her like he had. He listened to her and spoke to her like she mattered. He acted as if he had all the time in the world to stand there and answer her questions. She wished she had all the time in the world to listen. He made her feel safe. But she knew she had to go.

Bella sighed. No matter how much she wanted to experience the things Duncan had talked about, she still didn't understand how it all worked. And she hated to ask more questions than she already had. She didn't want him to figure her for stupid—if he hadn't already.

Maybe she *was* defective, as Andria had said earlier that morning. Maybe her mind didn't work in a way that would ever allow her to get close to God. She figured with her family background, her sins were bad enough that she'd never have that kind of relationship or closeness with Him. She'd been born a McLeod, and she'd die one. Momma had been a good person, and still, in the end, she'd been judged by her name alone.

Based on that, Bella didn't figure God would ever see past her many sins and give her Duncan's kind of hope and faith.

She consoled herself with the fact that the conversation wasn't a total waste. Now that they'd talked, Bella was pretty sure Duncan and the sheriff hadn't put together the McLeod connection. There was no way a good, upstanding man of God like Duncan would linger around on the public walkway, talking to a sinful member of the McLeod gang about Jesus if he had any idea of her true identity. If that was the case—if Duncan and Andrew had known who she and Andria were—surely they'd have arrested her and Andi on the spot and would have hauled 'em in for questioning. They might even have held them at the jail in the hope that the rest of the family would come into town to find them. Bella knew better than to believe that would ever happen. She and Andi were only of use when it came to helping in the hills. If they ever became a liability, they'd be dropped from the gang on the spot. Her brothers had no loyalty. She and Andria were expendable.

Now that she thought about it, Bella needed to figure out where Andria had wandered off to and round her up before she got herself into trouble. It was time to pick up their supplies. If they were to leave the pastor behind, they'd need to be on their way. She wanted enough daylight to make some serious progress before nightfall. She didn't want to travel the mountain trails in the dark of night.

She glanced over at the handsome man standing next to her. She was everything evil to his everything good. She needed to make her excuses and be on her way before Duncan saw through her guise and looked into the darkness that was her heart.

"I appreciate your time and kind words, Reverend Bowers. I'll take what you said to heart. But for now, I'd best collect my sister and be on my way."

He studied her a moment then nodded. "Where shall I meet you?"

She hesitated. "We're stayin' near Cooper's Creek, just outside of town. We'll leave from there." She felt bad deceiving the nice man. She didn't exactly lie—she just avoided telling the full truth by not disclosing *when* they planned to leave. Instead of leaving at first light, they'd leave long before. Still, she hated the fact that God could add another sin—a sin of omission—to the long list He probably already had on her. He probably didn't take too well to people betraying His pastors. This was just another confirmation for Bella that she'd never be good enough for God.

eight

"I can't believe you went into that establishment after I told you not to. I specifically told you not to go in there! The saloon isn't a place for someone like you to visit. It isn't a place anyone should visit. You're only seventeen. You don't belong in there. Oh! You exasperate me to no end." Bella hurried Andria along, anxious to broaden their distance from town. The whole town experience had bred nothing in her but dissatisfaction and frustration. "Just when I think we're gettin' somewhere, makin' plans for a new start, you defy me and do somethin' stupid. Saloons aren't safe, Andi. Why do I have to keep tellin' you that?"

"I was safe. You might not have noticed, Belle, but you're not my mother. You're not my father. You're my sister. I have a fine mind—you're always tellin' me that yourself—and based on that, I wish you could see that I can take care of myself. That includes making my own decisions. I wanted to find out if anyone would talk about a posse or talk about what's goin' on with that. I don't mean to be disrespectful, Bella, but you have no authority over me."

"That's quite obvious." Bella stalked ahead, furious at her sister's attitude. "Though in this messed-up clan that we call a family, I do have authority over you."

"Just like Wayne and Charlie have authority over us? That makes me want to *obey*, all right." Andria's words dripped with sarcasm. "And it seems to me, you aren't plannin' to *obey* much longer yourself. What makes it okay for you to refuse what they say or to plan against them?"

Bella lost some of her momentum. "That's not fair and you know it. What I do, I do in your best interest. I want you safe. Charlie and Wayne only use us for their future gain. They don't care about our well-bein' or safety. There's a huge difference."

Bella was at her wit's end. Earlier in the day it seemed she and her sister had gained some solid ground in their relationship, just to have her sister pull this. Now Andi was back to being her normal frustrating self. Bella sighed and slowed to a walk. "I don't want to see you hurt, Andi. I don't tell you things like this to irritate you."

"I'm not gonna get hurt, Bella."

"You don't know that. The men who hang out in those types of places aren't nice. You're far too young to be in there."

"I'm old enough to help our brothers make a livin'. I should be old enough to slip into a saloon and ask some questions."

"No, you aren't old enough to help our brothers. It's their responsibility to provide for us. Our brothers don't care about that, but I do. They shouldn't use you—or me—to do their biddin'. We've talked about this. We're going to make things right. Dallyin' in a saloon won't fix anything. That behavior will just create more problems."

They'd almost reached the clearing where they'd left their horses and supplies. Andria placed a hand on Bella's arm. Bella stopped and turned around to face her.

Andria closed her eyes and took a deep breath. "I'm sorry. I don't want us to fight. I just wanted to talk to someone besides family. I won't do it again."

Bella let out a sigh of relief. "Maybe you can get together

with Sarah soon. I know you miss visitin' with her."

Andi smiled.

"I do. I saw her awhile back, last time we went to Momma's cabin. But the visit was far too short." A look of guilt crossed her features. "I forgot, Bella. I did mention findin' some gold to her. I didn't tell her how much, but I showed her the three gold nuggets."

"Don't tell anyone else, and don't bring it up to her again."

"Maybe I should tell her next visit not to say anythin' to anyone else."

"Then we'll try to get there soon, after we clear everything up with the boys."

They picked up their pace and soon reached the area down by the water where they'd left their horses and belongings. Everything seemed to be as they'd left it earlier that morning.

"I told you this was a secure place." Bella beamed with relief. They'd found a small path leading away from the water they'd bathed in the night before, which led to another, smaller clearing. The second clearing ran alongside the creek. They'd set up camp and had left their things behind while they'd gone into town.

Andria stepped up beside her. "Are we still leavin' at first light? Or do you intend to sneak off in the night before your reverend comes to find you? If I have any say in this, I personally think we should stay the night and then get up early—that is—*if* you truly want to avoid him." Andria grinned.

"What do you mean 'if'? Of course I want to avoid him! And he's not 'my reverend.'" Bella stopped her tirade. Her voice was rising in pitch. She sounded guilty. She took a few breaths and calmed down. "We'll leave now. I want to get away from here long before he heads out to meet us. If we stayed through the night and overslept, he'd be hot on our heels all the way home."

Andria's face fell. Bella wondered if she had plans to sneak back into town or to do something equally nefarious. Her eyes narrowed. "You don't like that idea? What exactly did you have in mind that requires you to be near town?"

"Stop being so suspicious." Her sister shrugged. "The idea's all right, I guess. What I do like is that reverend. I think he likes you, too. I kind of hoped you'd relent and let him escort us home. I—for one—would appreciate the company."

Bella just gaped at her younger sister. The two years that separated them might as well have been decades. "He doesn't *like* me, Andria. He's a preacher. They have to be kind to everyone."

"Yes, but he seems to be *extra* kind to you. You never know. . .he might like you enough to stick around."

"Andria, a man like him—a man of God—isn't going to stay around for a woman like me."

"You could change."

"I *plan* to change. That's not the point."

"Then what is?" Andria folded her arms across her chest and waited for Bella's answer.

"I'm afraid if we come home in the company of Duncan, our brothers will try to kill him."

"I've never known them to be violent. Not like that."

"Were you not there yesterday morning when Wayne knocked me from my horse?"

"You know I was." Andria blushed. "But that was a random incident. You know better than to talk to Wayne that way." She appeared to rethink her words and hurried to add, "Not that that makes his actions right or anythin', but still, you know better than to confront him."

"What about the people he robs? You've never seen him

react violently when they refuse him?"

"I guess he has." Andria paled. "I've always tried to move forward and not give much thought about what happens after a robbery."

Bella was glad to see her sister still appeared to have a heart. No one should have to live like they did. They lived in constant fear of their brothers. Andria didn't like their life under their brothers' control any more than Bella did. "We're going to fix this. We're going to get out. But we won't use that kind man to make things any easier."

"I think he'd be willin'. I saw the way he looked at you."

"Andria! He's a *pastor!*"

"So?" Her sister laughed. "He's still a man. The whole time we were talkin' he couldn't take his eyes off you. And he looked at you like you were the most beautiful sight he'd ever seen."

"He did not, so just stop it." Bella knew she was blushing from head to toe. Her sister was spouting off crazy talk. Bella stalked over to the bushes and pulled her dry traveling clothes from the branches. She couldn't wait to put them on and leave the town behind. She tossed Andria's set to her. "Hurry up and change out of that dress and ready your horse for the trip."

"I'm more than happy to oblige. I'm ready to be out of these clothes. I've waited all day to get into somethin' more comfortable. I have no idea how women can get anythin' done in those constrictin' dresses."

"Most women don't ride the mountains and abandon angry victims like we do, Andi."

"I've never thought about that." Andria looked contemplative. "What do you suspect other women do all day anyhow?"

"I dunno. According to the books at Momma's place, they do things like bake, clean, and sew."

"How can that fill a whole day? I'd be bored out of my mind."

"I suppose I would be, too. But I'd sure like the chance to try it out and see. I think it would be relaxin' to sit out on the porch and look out over the mountains while darnin' socks and talkin' to my kin. You could while away the time as the sun sets on the horizon." Bella sighed. "Such a life would be peaceful and relaxin' for sure."

Andria stared at Bella as if she'd grown an extra head. "Darn a sock? How can you imagine sittin' there doin' somethin' you hardly ever do?"

Bella smiled. "The darnin' isn't what's important. I'm just sayin'. . .we've never had the opportunity to live a normal life like that. We've never had the chance to do domestic things and enjoy the easy life most other women live. Seems to me it'd be a nice way to fiddle away our time."

"I dunno. I've seen Sarah's mom goin' about her chores, and they look pretty hard to me. She's always doin' somethin' or other and hardly gets a moment to rest. Momma used to work pretty hard, too."

Bella shrugged. "I'd prefer to settle in and take the time to really see what's happenin' around me. It isn't any fun to always be lookin' over our shoulders, wonderin' when the law's gonna catch up with us. Domestic life would set right well with me."

"You have a point. I guess it would be a nice way to live, sittin' around doin' nothin'." Andria looked at the garment in her arm. "Maybe I'd even enjoy wearing the likes of this dress if we had a life like that. You have to admit, the dresses were cooler than these pants once we figured out how to wear 'em."

"Yes, they were." Bella slipped into her pants and finished dressing for the trail. The dress was definitely cooler, but the pants allowed them more freedom of movement while on the trail. The trail they were now ready to follow so they could get themselves far away from town—and Duncan.

❧

Duncan grinned as he watched the McLeod women ride out of the clearing at a fast pace. He'd been sure Bella would try to give him the slip, but Andrew said after watching them talk in town, he thought Bella would wait around for her escort. Duncan had hurried home to pack, just to be on the safe side, and it looked like his precaution paid off.

From all appearances, it seemed Andrew had lost their bet and would owe Duncan a dinner next time they met up. Duncan decided to tail the women at a distance for a while. He'd make his presence known after they'd gained some ground. It'd go better for him if he followed them with discretion. No need to get them all riled up and angry if he could avoid it. He could watch out for them just as well from afar as he could if he rode along with them.

In all honesty, he'd probably keep his focus on protecting them better from way back here. Bella had a way of distracting him, and he couldn't afford that. If she wasn't distracting him with her rare but pretty smile, she'd be arguing with him. He couldn't afford to be caught off guard if and when they met up with her brothers.

The women were skilled on horseback. They moved at a fast clip, making it hard for Duncan to keep up, watch his surroundings, and keep out of sight. He wondered if they'd try to ride all night or if they'd pull off at dusk. He'd have a harder time following them at night.

The sun was low on the horizon when Bella and Andria ducked into a stand of trees and disappeared from sight. Relieved, Duncan slowly made his way in that direction. He didn't want to ride all night. He wanted to catch some sleep so he'd be fresh for whatever Bella's homecoming brought along with it.

He heard their voices as they moved about setting up camp. He debated whether he should quietly settle in nearby or if he should make his presence known. Since they'd so casually stopped off where they had and didn't seem to give a thought to their surroundings or safety, he decided to alert them to his presence and let them know they weren't as observant as they thought.

He left the trail and burst through the thick trees and into their encampment. Both women screamed.

Duncan tipped his hat and gave them his most cocky grin. "Evenin', ladies. Seems y'all left somethin' behind."

The women spun around with weapons raised. Andria had snatched up a nearby log, while Bella had her rifle trained on him.

"Whoa, it's just me!" Duncan raised his arms.

They stood and stared at him for a few moments before recognizing him and lowering the weapons. Bella leaned against hers and glowered while Andria stood with a hand to her heart. Andria looked as if she'd seen a ghost while Bella returned his cocky glance and looked over at their belongings. "I don't see anything of importance missin', Andria, do you? Whatever could we have forgotten, Reverend Bowers?"

"Me."

Bella rolled her eyes. "In order to 'forget' you, I would have had to plan to bring you along in the first place. In case you didn't notice, I didn't plan any such thing."

Duncan feigned shock. "You didn't plan to bring me along? You snuck out of there without me on purpose? I thought it was an oversight."

"My only oversight was leavin' without checkin' things

out better. And there was no sneakin' involved. We merely changed our plans and decided to make some progress while we had daylight to burn."

"I've been meaning to talk to you about that."

"About burnin' daylight?"

"About leaving without checking things out better."

"How much time could you possibly have had to 'mean to talk' to me about anythin'? You've only been here a few moments."

"Thought-filled moments. And I've followed you for hours since you ducked away from town while trying to dodge me."

"And yet here you stand."

"Obviously, your efforts were in vain."

"I can see that. Thanks for fillin' me in."

Andria stood a few feet away from them, still holding on to her log, looking from one to the other as they continued their verbal sparring. "Are y'all 'bout done?"

Duncan glanced over at Bella.

Bella shrugged.

"Guess so."

"Yep."

Andria dropped the log. "Well then, now that we have that all figured out, maybe we can finish figurin' out the important things like settin' up camp before night falls?"

"Sounds like a plan." Duncan looked around for something that needed his attention. "What would you like me to do?"

Bella sighed dramatically. "What *I'd* like you to do is—"

"Why don't you start us a nice fire, Reverend Bowers? We'll finish up our other preparations in the meantime."

"I don't need to be referred to as Reverend Bowers, Andria. Duncan will do just fine. I don't go on formalities, especially way out here."

Bella spoke before Andria had a chance. "So we noticed when you pranced in here all arrogant-like on your high horse."

Duncan laughed. "Since when did being a pastor mean you couldn't be comfortable with those around you? It seems I bring more people to my side by making them feel at ease than I do while standing in judgment."

Bella didn't comment; she just stood and stewed. Andria grabbed her sister by the arm and dragged her away from his side. Duncan couldn't hear what they were saying, but he could hear the anger in Bella's voice.

After a few minutes, they'd apparently reached a mutual decision because both walked over to join him. Bella didn't look any less angry, but she went about her business as he prepared the finishing touches for their fire.

"I hope you brought along your own food. I didn't pack enough for an extra person." Bella's words were a mix of irritation and apology.

"I'll be fine. Don't worry about me. I'm here to help, not to hinder."

"Then you should've stayed behind," Bella muttered.

Though she first appeared to be angry, Duncan noticed an undercurrent of panic in her voice. He felt bad that his presence caused her frustration.

Andria glanced up at him to gauge his reaction. He winked at her before turning to Bella. Andria's eyes widened in surprise.

"I couldn't do that, Bella. I know you're upset with me for following you. You have every right to be offended. But Sheriff Andrew and I both felt we needed to make sure you reached your home in a safe manner. We'd never forgive ourselves if we found out something had happened to you on the trail. Something my presence could have prevented."

"Yes, because men of cloth are known to be such good gunfighters in battle. What can you possibly do for us that we can't do for ourselves? If you get hurt because of us, *we'll* be the ones who can't forgive ourselves."

"You owe me nothing, and I take responsibility for my own choices. I had a life out in these hills, Bella, before I decided to live for the Lord. I've dealt with the likes of those who live out this way. I've worked with Andrew in various situations, and I've had to lay down the law for those on the wrong side of the badge more than once. You just say the word once I have you safely home, and I'll leave."

Bella looked at him with indecision. Whether she was debating taking him up on his offer or still trying to figure out how to send him packing, Duncan didn't know. She had a cantankerous look about her that said her mind wouldn't stop when it came to thinking up ways to lose him again as soon as she could. "I don't see that I have any choice in the matter."

Duncan felt bad. Maybe he should have stayed out of sight and just followed them in without their ever knowing.

The irritable spark in Bella's eyes grew larger. "You know what? We could've had you tied up and lyin' flat on the ground if we'd wanted to. We went easy on you because of who you are."

Andria's mouth twitched.

Duncan stared at them, incredulous. "You're tellin' me you knew I was back there all along?" He laughed. "If that were the case, why didn't you let me know? Why did you look so startled when I walked into the clearing? I don't believe it."

Bella shrugged. "We didn't want to make you feel bad."

For a moment, Duncan didn't know whether or not he

should believe them. He finally decided it didn't really matter. Not as much as it mattered that he was able to accompany them home. He needed to make peace.

"It seems like you have everything under control. What's the plan for tomorrow?"

"We'll get up early and head out first thing. You'll need to choose a spot far away from us when you go to sleep. I don't wanna have to worry about the snoring keepin' anyone up."

"Aw, your snores can't be all that bad. I'm sure they won't bother me a bit. I'm a heavy sleeper."

"I wasn't talking about *my* snoring botherin' *you*, I was talking about *your* snoring botherin' *us*!" Bella huffed.

"So you do snore?"

"No! I do not."

Andria tried to hide her laughter behind her hand.

Duncan turned to her. "Andria, does Bella snore?"

"Not often, and not real loud or anything. Her snores are more like quiet little snuffles."

"I don't snore!" Bella's horrified screech made Duncan laugh.

He asked, "What makes you think I snore?"

"Don't all men? My father and. . ." Her voice drifted off. "Other family members have snored. I've heard them all the way from the barn to the house."

"That doesn't mean all men snore."

"Well maybe not, then. But all the same, you need to sleep far away from here. I don't want to hear you or know you're nearby."

"I bet if you hear a large bear rustling around in the trees you'll want me nearby soon enough."

"The only sound of a bear rustlin' in the trees will be you tryin' to scare us."

"I'd never do anything of the sort." He softened his voice, wanting her to know the teasing was over and he meant the statement. "I'll stay out of your way, but I'll be close enough to help if you run into trouble."

nine

A rustling in the nearby trees moments later had Duncan on alert and reaching for his rifle. Andria stepped closer to Bella. Bella held her own rifle at the ready.

"Whoever you are, make your presence known."

Duncan's strong voice at Bella's side made her jump. She had a momentary vision of a large black bear rushing out of the woods with paws raised in fear. Instead, a small boy with unruly red hair and a scowl on his face slowly walked out of the thick stand of trees and moved into the clearing. His green eyes reflected in the firelight as he surveyed the three adults gathered around the blaze.

"Ethan?" Duncan roared. He lowered his rifle. "What on earth do you think you're doing following me around like this and wandering through the woods? You almost got yourself shot."

"I knew you wouldn't shoot me."

"You're right, Ethan. I wouldn't knowingly shoot me. But I didn't *know* it was you, did I? I was expecting a bear or an outlaw to walk out of those trees, not you."

Ethan looked from Duncan to Bella to Andria. "What are you doin' out here all alone with these two women? I thought preachers weren't supposed to do things like that."

"Do things like what?" Duncan looked confused.

"Be alone with strange women in the woods."

"I'm protecting them from bears and outlaws," Duncan muttered. "Your father wanted me to chaperone them and keep them safe until they reached their home."

Bella couldn't help but laugh.

Duncan turned his stormy expression on her. "You find this situation to be amusing?"

"No." Bella tried to corral her emotions. "It's just that you were standin' here not too long ago lecturing us about being more observant and how we needed to be aware of our surroundin's, and yet this small boy apparently followed you all the way from town without your knowledge. Just seems a bit ironic is all."

"I was focused on keeping you safe."

"I ain't small," Ethan sputtered.

"I didn't mean any offense," Bella hurried to say, trying to tamp down her amusement. "To either of you."

She had to admit it was nice of Duncan to watch out for their well-being. Her brothers certainly hadn't ever concerned themselves with such a thing. But Bella couldn't keep her jaded thoughts from wondering what Duncan's ulterior motive was. In Bella's experience, all men had one.

She hoped the preacher proved her wrong, but she wouldn't count on it.

"Come on over to the fire." Bella wrapped an arm around Ethan's shoulder. "I bet you're pretty hungry after all that ridin'. We'll see if we can find you something to eat."

"What?" Duncan widened his arms. "I'm here on your behalf, with the best of intentions, and all I get is yelled at, threatened, and told that I won't be eating. Ethan walks in here unannounced when he shouldn't be here at all, scares us all to death, and you welcome him with open arms?"

"He's just a boy. His parents must be worried sick."

"She has a point." Duncan turned suspicious eyes toward the boy. "What did you tell your parents?"

Ethan dug his toe in the dirt. "I didn't exactly tell them anythin'."

"Ethan! Argh!" Duncan threw his hat on the ground. "Now I have to turn around and take you back to town. I needed to escort these ladies to their homestead, but thanks to you, they're going to be unsafe for the rest of the trip while I tend to you."

Bella's heart trilled. The precious little boy had fixed their dilemma. Thanks to him they'd be able to return home with no worries when it came to their brothers hurting Duncan.

Ethan bristled. "You don't have to take me back. My ma went to visit her sister and won't be back for at least a week. She told me to stay home with my pa."

"And you don't think your pa will be upset to find you missing?" Duncan asked. "Ethan, you've really messed up this time. Didn't we just talk in town this morning about respecting others?"

"I thought we talked about stealin'." Ethan looked confused.

"It's all one and the same. Stealing from someone causes them frustration and makes them upset. Leaving town without telling your pa or ma will cause them frustration. They'll be worried."

"No they won't. Pa thinks I went with Ma. That was the original plan. That is—it was the plan before she went and got all upset with me for killin' her precious flower bushes."

Duncan sat on a nearby rock and rested his forehead on his hand. "Maybe you'd better start at the beginning."

"Ma and I were supposed to go visit her sister, my Aunt Maggie. Aunt Maggie smells like dead weeds, and her cookin' makes me wish I was sick in bed."

Andria unsuccessfully choked back a laugh. Bella nudged her, doing a better job at hiding her own amusement this round.

"Ma told me to dump her cleanin' water. I thought she'd used it to wash dishes, so I threw it on the plants. They all wilted and died. Apparently it wasn't from the dishes after all."

Duncan rubbed his hand across the back of his neck. "Apparently not."

"So, Ma got mad and said I could just stay home with my pa. She was tired of my antics. She muttered something about it being good for the both of us."

"I can only imagine." Duncan studied the young boy for a moment. "So what's your pa gonna think when he comes home to find you gone?"

Ethan's face lit up. "That's the good part! I never did get around to tellin' my pa before I saw you sneakin' out of town. I decided to follow along—since I was in trouble anyway—and see where you was goin'."

"I wasn't 'sneaking,' Ethan. I told you, your pa wanted me to escort these ladies and keep them safe."

"Sure looked like sneakin' to me."

"Well it wasn't."

"Then why did you keep close to the trees and hang back when the ladies slowed their pace?"

Bella laughed out loud this time. Duncan sent her a very unpreacher-like glare.

"I wanted to make sure the ladies were safe without interfering with their trip."

"Like we're doin' now?" Ethan quipped.

"Exactly like you're doing now," Bella agreed.

"How can we be interfering with your trip when you aren't traveling?" Duncan asked.

He had a point.

"You're interferin' with our dinner preparations," Bella responded.

"Would you like me to leave?"

"No." Bella took pity on him. "I'd actually like for you to join us. I know it doesn't seem like it, but we do appreciate your concern for our well-bein'—misguided though it might be."

"So we're stayin'?" Ethan's face lit up.

"For dinner," Duncan answered. "After that, we'll head back so I can return you to your father."

"What if my father isn't there when you return me?"

Duncan closed his eyes. "What aren't you telling me now?"

"Pa got called out of town on business. He'll be gone for several days, too."

"And when did you find this out? After your ma left and before you took off after me?"

Ethan's brows furrowed with deep thought. "After my ma left, but before I took off after you. Yes." He glanced up to see Duncan's glower and hurried on with his story. "I saddled up my horse and was ready to go after you when I saw my dad talkin' to some men and I hid in the alley so he wouldn't see me. I heard them say they were goin' after someone and wouldn't be back for at least a few days. My pa said that was all right and he'd go along because me and my ma were out of town anyway."

"So no one will miss you for at least a week?"

"Right. Not until my ma comes home."

"Where's your horse now?"

"I tied him to a tree outside the clearing so you wouldn't hear me ride up."

Duncan looked thoughtful. "So we have time to escort the ladies back to their homestead and then get home in plenty of time to tell your pa."

Ethan wrinkled his nose at that. "He won't be too happy about that."

"No, I don't imagine he'll be happy at all, but that's the price you have to pay for your deception and disrespect." He grinned at Bella. "And in the meantime, I'll still be able to follow through on my commitment to help these ladies reach their home."

&

Bella rode her horse into the open area around the homestead midmorning the following day. She exchanged an uneasy glance with Andria.

"I sure hope this plan works, Belle."

"So do I. But it seemed like the best idea at the time."

Bella knew her brothers would show up eventually. She hoped Duncan and Ethan would be long gone before then. She and Andi had stayed up late, trying to figure out the best approach for the trip home. Their final decision was to visit their mother's homestead under the assumption that it was their permanent home.

Duncan rode up behind them. "You have a beautiful place here."

The homestead overlooked the Blue Ridge Mountains. From where they sat upon their horses, the mountains rolled away into the distance. Early morning mist hung in the valleys and swirled around them in the yard. The songbirds were well into their singing, the different varieties melding together from the treetops above their heads. The fresh scent of jasmine blew around them on the breeze. It was a magical place.

"Thank you. We love it here." The statement couldn't be any truer. She'd loved their years growing up here before Momma took sick and died. She loved the times their brothers sent them over to wait out whatever was going on in the hills after a robbery. She dreamed of the day they could settle in at the homestead without the fear of their brothers arriving and wreaking havoc.

"I can see why." He smiled. "I feel closer to God up here. There aren't any distractions like I have in town. Up here it's just God and His creation."

Funny, Bella thought, *I've never felt further away from God.*

Most likely because of all the sad family memories, the bad times, the fear she felt during their brothers' escapades. Though the cabin was a refuge, it also bore scars of past hurts. And if Duncan only knew, all kinds of distractions to his peace were waiting just around the corner.

"I wish I felt the same way. But then, I don't feel close to God no matter where I go."

Duncan studied her. The intensity of his probing eyes caused her discomfort. She shifted in her saddle.

"You could if you'd just let Him into your heart. Give Him control of your life."

Bella laughed, the sound harsh as it drifted away like the mist. "You don't understand. Some people don't have the ability to make such a choice."

"Everyone has that ability."

"Not me."

"Yes you. All you have to do is ask."

"Such a thing would completely turn my life upside down. I can't let that happen."

Duncan's expression grew troubled. "Tell me what the problem is. Maybe I can help."

Bella gentled her words with a smile. "No one can help, but I appreciate your concern."

She ended the conversation by dropping from her horse and following Andi into the cabin. The room was dark and dreary. It smelled musty and unused. She left the door open as Andi rushed over to open the opposite door that looked out over the backyard. Light trickled in and brightened the area.

Duncan appeared in the doorway. "I sent Ethan over to the barn with the horses. He'll take good care of them."

"I can help!" Andria seemed all too eager to steer clear of Duncan's presence.

Bella watched as Duncan circled the untidy room. Layers of dust covered every surface.

"I'm not much for housekeeping. You'll have to excuse the mess."

He raised an eyebrow in reply. She knew it was an understatement. The house hadn't been lived in for several years, and she and Andria didn't see much reason to clean it during their brief visits.

Duncan ran his fingers over the titles of the books on the shelves. "Looks like someone liked to read."

"Our mother did. She loved to read. She taught school back East before her father brought the family out here for the Georgia gold rush."

"Did he find gold?"

"No, and he died before he could be lured farther west after his claim fizzled out. Momma met our pa, and she settled in here at the homestead."

"Where's she now?"

"She passed away a few years ago."

"I'm sorry to hear that. And your father?"

"He passed away, too. After Momma died he started to drink all the time. I think it ruined his health."

"Liquor can do that to a person." Sympathy filled his eyes. "So your brothers took over your care?"

"We were old enough to care for ourselves, but yes, they

took on watchin' over us."

Duncan stopped in front of the family Bible. A layer of dust rested upon the sacred cover. He blew it off and looked over at Bella. "I take it no one around here reads the Good Book?"

"Um, not lately."

Their mother had been the last to open the cover of the large book. Her brothers would rather toss the thing into a bonfire than to ever read a word of what lay inside. Though their mother had tried to read the scriptures aloud to her wayward children, her words had fallen upon dry ground. Bella wished she'd been older. She and Andria had been too young to understand back then, and when they were old enough to understand, their mother's breath was too precious to waste with reading.

Duncan opened the book to the page that listed their names and dates of birth. He studied them carefully then frowned. Bella's heart beat loudly in her chest. What would he do when he saw her brothers' names inscribed on the pages of that fine book? Their names didn't even deserve to be located in such a special place. She was sure her own name and Andria's were just as poorly placed.

"You don't have a brother named Alex?"

"No." Confused, Bella shook her head. "Just my sister, Alexandria, but we've always called her Andria or Andi. Why do you ask?"

"I heard the name mentioned in passing. I figured with you being a McLeod, he might be a relative of yours."

Duncan didn't say another word as he closed the book and continued his trek around the room. "The dust around here is mostly untouched. You must not spend much time indoors."

Bella realized her mistake. If they lived at the cabin, it would be clean and tidy. Instead, as he said, the layers of dust coated everything in the room. She and Andria never stayed long when they were sent to the cabin. They gathered whatever items they'd been sent to claim, or they worked around the yard until one of their brothers sent for them.

"With a view like we have outside, would you? It's much better outside with the fresh air and sunshine. But if you must know, the dust gathers fast up here in the mountains."

"It does, does it?" Duncan's mouth turned up at the corners.

Bella couldn't tell if he was laughing at her or if he took her words to heart. She motioned toward the front of the house. "As you can see, we like to keep the doors open for all the light it brings in. The practice comes with a price."

She hurried over to the corner and picked up a worn broom. "I'll tidy up if it'll make you feel better. I don't want you thinkin' poorly of us. We do know how to clean." She placed the broom on the ground and started to sweep with it. The rotted handle promptly broke in half. Bella couldn't do anything but stare at the defective item.

"You've worn that poor broom to a frazzle with all your cleaning up." Duncan laughed. "I'll tell you what. Let me make you a new handle and you can resume your—cleaning—as soon as I get it done."

Bella felt the flush crawl up her neck but refused to back down. "I'd be mighty obliged to you if you did that. Thank you."

He stepped from the room, and Bella sank into her mother's rocking chair with frustration. Dust motes danced in the shafts of sunlight that filtered in through the front door. Now her deception not only had her hiding her brothers' identity, but it also had her pretending to be something she wasn't.

Andria walked into the room. "Duncan said something about making us a new broom?" She looked around. "I didn't even realize we had an old one."

Bella buried her face in her hands. "I know. I didn't realize we had one, either. He started talkin' about the condition of the place, and I saw the broom hidin' in that corner over there. I picked it up, and it broke to pieces in my hand. I suppose he knows we're tryin' to trick him into thinkin' we live here. I mean, look at this place!"

Andria looked it over. "It is pretty rough. Momma would be ashamed."

"We'll start today and clean it in a way that would make her proud. From now on when we're sent over to wait things out, we'll make use of the time and keep it up to her standards. No more idle hands for us."

Andi nodded her agreement. "I hate to bring this up, but we have another dilemma."

"Which is. . . ?"

"We have no food to offer them. We have no chickens to lay eggs, no cow to milk, not much grain for all the horses. . . . Don't you think they'll figure out—if they haven't already— that no one has lived here in a long, long time?"

"We have the supplies we brought from town. I know it's not much, but surely they'll realize two women on their own wouldn't have need for a lot of supplies?" She thought a moment. "Perhaps you can run over to Sarah's and buy a couple of chickens from her parents? They used to breed them. I would imagine they still do. Perhaps they'll even loan us a goat for a few days. Tell them we're workin' on fixin' up Momma's place."

Andria's face brightened at the thought. "I'd love to go over there! Sarah will be so excited to know I'm back again."

"Don't get too excited, Andi. You know this is only for a short time. We'll be able to send Duncan off before we know it, and we'll need to head back to the other homestead."

Andria's face fell. "I know. You're right. But for a moment there, I got carried away with the thought of stayin' and fixin' the old place up. It's so much warmer and homier than the other cabin. I hate it there."

"I hate it there, too. We'll be here soon. I promise. And the more we can do now to get it in shape, the better it'll be when we return."

Bella just hoped her promise was one she could keep.

ten

Duncan watched as Andria hurried off into the trees on foot. The hair raised on the back of his neck. He hoped she wasn't going to warn her brothers about their arrival. He couldn't risk Ethan's safety. He'd need to act fast if the rest of the McLeod gang arrived unexpectedly. He couldn't imagine that Bella or Andria would set them up, but one never knew. They seemed genuine, but he'd seen outlaws turn for all sorts of reasons. Number one reason for the McLeod women to betray him was that they were terrified of their older brothers. Or at least that was the impression Duncan had received when listening in to their conversation the day he'd first met up with them.

He finished up the final touches on the new broom and tested it on the dirt floor of the empty barn. It seemed to sweep just fine. He headed for the house. Bella puttered around, tidying up the kitchen area.

"I just saw Andria head off into the woods. Is everything all right?"

Bella nodded but didn't look him in the eye or stop wiping the table with the old rag she clutched tightly in her hand. "She's going over to retrieve our livestock from a neighbor's house."

"You take your livestock to a friend's when you leave for a couple of days?"

"We don't have anyone who can come over and care for them."

She didn't elaborate further.

"I have your broom ready to go. Care to give it a try?"

"Sure. I'd love to." Bella finally turned his way, her nose wrinkled with disdain, telling him the opposite was true. She was too polite to tell him that, of course, but her actions made it clear. It was obvious housework wasn't her strong suit. Based on her favorite choice of clothes and her independent ways, he figured she didn't have much experience with housework in general. The cabin's condition attested to that. It looked to him like nobody had lived in the house for quite some time.

"As soon as I'm done sweepin', I'll start the fire and get somethin' goin' for the noon meal." She said this with a tone of resignation. She eyed the stove with dislike. "I suppose I'll need some wood."

"I'll get it for you. Just tell me where to find it." Duncan hadn't noticed any wood stacked anywhere around the grounds, but he hadn't exactly been looking.

"Tell you where the wood is? Oh. . ." Bella looked nervous. "I believe we might have used the last of it before we left on the trip."

"You must travel a lot."

"More than I'd like to, yes."

He moved to the door. "I'll see what I can find. Where would I find an ax?"

She frowned. "Perhaps we have one in the barn?"

The comment was more question than statement. Duncan had a distinct feeling Bella and Andria were up to something. He wondered if the place was even theirs. He remembered their names in the family Bible and figured they had some tie to the cabin. But he also knew they could have planted the Bible there at some point. Or maybe the cabin had belonged to their grandparents.

Duncan still had concerns about Andria's disappearance. He kept one eye on the trees while he looked around for an ax. He sent Ethan out to look behind the barn, and Ethan called out that he'd found one. Duncan hurried around the small structure and found the ax buried deep into a tree stump. Judging by the amount of rust on the head, it had been sitting there for a long, long time. He tried to pull it out, but it had become permanently embedded into the wood. Ethan grinned, pleased that he'd been the one to find it.

"Want me to chop the wood for you, Duncan? I can help out that way."

"Thanks, Ethan, but I think you'd do better finding us some wood to cut once I get the ax in working condition. While you're at it, gather up some smaller pieces to use as kindling."

"All right." Ethan's face fell.

"We can't have a fire without wood, Ethan. Finding the wood is every bit as important as cutting it."

"Yes, sir."

"I have to work on this ax for a while before it'll be usable anyway, if it ever will be."

"Yeah. Those ladies should put their equipment away before they leave for town next time."

Duncan nodded his agreement but didn't tell the boy that the ax had obviously been there for years, not days.

Bella walked through the rear barn door and entered the shady clearing that surrounded the back of it. "You found the ax. Good."

"What's left of it anyway. I'll have to see if I can make it usable again. How long has it been since you two had wood anyway? How have you survived here, Bella?"

❧

Duncan's concern made Bella feel even guiltier about their deception. She reminded herself that the deception was necessary for everyone's well-being. "We make do all right. Our neighbors are good people. We all watch out for each other." Which at least was true back before her momma had died.

Duncan looked relieved. "So the neighbors bring you wood for the fire. That would make sense. I'm glad to know you have people watching out for you."

"Right." The only people who had ever watched out for Bella and Andria since their mother passed away were standing right in front of her. Sarah's family had tried to talk Bella's father into letting Bella and Andria move in with them, but their father wouldn't hear of it.

"Are they due to bring more wood soon?"

"Um. I'm not sure." Bella hated this situation. She wished Duncan would leave so they could stop the farce. "We'll be fine though until they do. You and Ethan can be on your way. I don't want his father to worry."

"You heard the boy. His father won't be home for another week at the earliest. I don't have to preach again until Sunday. And I have an arrangement in place so that if I can't get back in time to preach on a given Sunday, a friend in town will cover the service for me. If he doesn't hear from me by Saturday afternoon, he knows he's to step in and preach the next sermon."

"How wonderful." She didn't bother to hide her sarcasm. What were they to do now? Her brothers would show up sooner or later, and they'd turn the place upside down. She couldn't bear it if Ethan or Duncan got hurt. She hadn't known them long, but she related to Ethan more than he knew and she found Duncan's overprotective ways to be endearing. She figured if she told him the truth he'd refuse to leave and would face her oldest brother's wrath. She knew Duncan couldn't stay forever, but she knew she could learn from his presence if she could only spend a little bit more time with him.

"You don't sound very enthusiastic."

"As I've tried to tell you, Andria and I have been on our own for quite a while. We aren't used to anyone else lookin' out for us. I hate for you to miss out on your own obligations while we start gettin' used to dependin' on someone else."

Confusion clouded Duncan's features. "Then you don't have supportive neighbors?"

"We do. . .when we're here. Which isn't often. Which you've probably already figured out."

"Often being—every few years?"

Bella shrugged. "Somethin' like that."

"If you don't mind my asking, where do you live the rest of the time?"

"I can't answer that. I wish I could. We live a solitary life. We're not used to dealing with outsiders." At least that part was the truth. The sad truth.

"Do you want us to leave?"

A heavy feeling settled over Bella at the thought. She did and she didn't want him to leave. She wanted him and Ethan far away from her brothers. But she also wanted to spend more time with him. He'd forced his presence upon them, but he'd been nothing but a gentleman and she longed to know more about him and his relationship with God. She knew she could never tell him about her brothers, but she didn't want to lose the tenuous relationship they were building. Preacher or not, he was the first kind man she had ever known.

She corrected herself. Sarah's father was kind, but he'd been more of a father figure to them back when they were young. He'd tried to step in when her father's manner changed. He'd talked to her brothers when they'd started running wild. That's when they'd moved the girls up to the other homestead.

Duncan, on the other hand, seemed more of a friend, even though she barely knew him. She knew he had to be kind to everyone, his position required it, but it was still nice to know someone cared and was watching out for them.

"I'm sure I should say that I do want you to leave, but in all honesty, I don't. Not yet."

"Ah, you want us to stay and help you put the cabin back in order, is that it?" Duncan teased.

"No. Yes. I mean. . .I'd love to have you help with the cabin. But I also appreciate your concern and the escort and your offer of help. I don't want to take advantage, but it's nice to have someone here watchin' out for us. It's nice to feel safe." She closed her eyes in mortification. She'd said too much. It was one thing to think the words, something entirely different to utter them to his face.

"You aren't taking advantage, Bella. I offered, remember? I wouldn't have offered my help if I hadn't meant it."

"I know."

Duncan leaned against the ax handle. The head was still stuck tight into the stump. "Who or what do you need to feel safe from? Being alone? Because as I said, God is a great companion. Or is there something more that you're afraid of? Because God can help there, too."

"I'm sorry. I shouldn't be talkin' to you about this." Bella turned on her heel and hurried back to the house. She should have told him to go ahead and leave. It would only be harder to see him go, the longer he was there. And he hadn't been there very long as it was. Something deep inside drew her to him. She figured it was her desire to know God, but there was something more, too.

She shook her head. It was probably nothing more than panic over her brothers' possible actions and pure terror at the thought of being alone with them again. She knew she was headed for a confrontation with them, and she didn't relish the thought. She knew she could no longer help them with their outlawin' ways. There'd most definitely be a confrontation.

Having a strong man like Duncan at her side when that day came would do wonders for her confidence when facing them, but was it fair to bring him in? She needed to warn him, but she knew he'd leave.

She and Andria had the little matter of the gold to deal with, too. If her brothers became suspicious about Bella's loyalty, they'd never leave them alone long enough to claim the fortune. The fortune that was their ticket out of their brothers' clutches.

Ethan had carried in the supplies when they'd first arrived home and had laid them just inside the door. Bella went over and dug through the parcels, trying to figure out what to make for dinner. She glanced out the window and saw Andria walk through the trees with Sarah by her side.

"Sarah!" Bella laid the supplies on the table and rushed out to meet her sister's childhood friend. Though Sarah was closer to Andria in age, all three had played together.

Sarah pulled her into a warm hug, turning sideways so as not to knock Bella over with the large bag she carried over her shoulder. "Momma sent over some food for you. I came along to help Andi with the animals." She glanced around. "Not that I see a place for you to put the hens."

"I'll figure something out." Duncan walked up to join them. He looked relieved to see Andria. "Nice cages."

"My dad rigged them up for us." Sarah laughed. "I'm Sarah."

"Pleased to meet you, Sarah. I'm Duncan."

The goat butted Andria in the thigh. She squealed and handed the rope over to Duncan.

Duncan took it with a laugh and led the ornery goat off toward the barn. "Bring the hens to the barn when you get through chatting."

Sarah turned to Andria and said in a loud whisper. "You were right—he is handsome."

"Andria!" Bella looked at Duncan's retreating back for a sign that he'd heard Sarah's declaration.

He didn't miss a step.

"I was just fillin' her in. It's not like it isn't true. You have to admit he's easy on the eye."

"I've never denied it, but he's a pastor. You need to speak of him with respect."

"How is sayin' he's handsome disrespectful? In case you didn't notice, it's a compliment, Belle."

"It is a compliment, but still, you mustn't talk that way about him."

"Pastors marry, too, Bella," Sarah joined in.

"I know. But you need to remember and respect his position."

Sarah went on as if Bella hadn't spoken. "I, for one, wouldn't mind bein' a pastor's wife if I could marry one that looked as fine as he does."

"Absolutely not. Get that thought right out of your head."

"I'm not allowed to marry a pastor?"

"You're not allowed to think about marrying this pastor."

Sarah sighed. "So no hanging on his arm, begging for a walk around the property?"

"Goodness no! Especially not anythin' like that." Bella surprised herself as feelings of jealousy reared to life. She had no hold on Duncan.

Sarah and Andria laughed.

Bella had a feeling she'd been set up. "You two need to get those hens out to Duncan and ask him to come in for the noon meal. Round up Ethan while you're out there. Is there enough food here for everyone?"

"Momma asked how many you had at the cabin. There's plenty of food for everyone, myself included." Her enthusiasm slowed. "That is, if you don't mind my stayin'. I can leave if you'd rather."

"Of course I'd love for you to stay. Andi has missed you so much."

"And you haven't?"

"I certainly have." She gave Sarah an extra hug for good measure.

"Any chance y'all are back for good?"

Bella sent Andria a warning glare. "Not for now. Maybe someday soon, though."

Sarah's face fell. "I miss havin' y'all nearby. It's been too long."

"I know. We want to come home, too. But we have to be with our brothers for now. Speakin' of,"—she glanced over toward the barn—"for the time being, can you not mention them?"

"Why?"

"Duncan doesn't know about them, and I feel it's best to keep it that way. I don't want him asking too many questions."

"He doesn't know about them?"

"He knows we have brothers. He doesn't know what they do."

"So it's true what they say." Sarah looked upset.

"What who says?" Bella had a bad feeling in the pit of her stomach.

"The locals. Word gets around. You know how it is out here." Sarah motioned toward the hills over her shoulder.

"Yes, I know."

"Rumor has it, your brothers are the ones ridin' the hills and robbin' folks. I didn't want to believe it. They said they call themselves the McLeod gang."

"They don't call themselves anything," Bella stated. "And Andria and I are tryin' to figure out exactly what's going on with them. Until we do, please promise you won't say anythin' to anyone about our being here or about Wayne and Charlie while you're around Duncan."

"I promise. I'll keep your secret."

Bella hoped she would.

eleven

Dinner was a noisy occasion with Ethan at the table. The young boy never quieted, even as he ate bites of his food. Duncan was forever correcting him, telling him not to talk with his mouth full; but a moment later, Ethan was asking a question or sharing a story with anyone who'd listen.

Bella picked up the basket of bread and passed it around. Sarah's mother had thought of everything, down to the butter for the bread. The slices of cured ham set Bella's mouth to watering. She hadn't had food like this in years. Not since her mother had been well enough to cook. Their meal in town had smelled wonderful, but she'd been so nervous that day, sitting next to Duncan and the sheriff, that she couldn't enjoy the food. She'd been too worried that they'd figure out her relationship to Wayne and Charlie.

She used a fork to pull two slices of ham onto her plate. She reached for the butter and spread it across the bread. The bread was still warm and melted the butter as soon as she slathered it on. Green beans, fresh from Sarah's family's garden, rounded out the fine meal. Bella decided then and there she'd plant fresh vegetables as soon as she and Andria settled down.

She placed a hand on Sarah's. "Sarah, please tell your mother thank you for the meal. It's wonderful. I haven't had food as good as this in a long, long time."

Duncan grunted his agreement.

"You know how Momma is. She wanted you to come over

and eat at our place, but Andria said you'd just arrived and couldn't leave just yet."

"Andi is right. The place is a shambles, and we have a lot to do. I think Duncan has decided to stick around a few days and help us out."

"That's very nice of you." Sarah batted her eyes at him.

Duncan smiled back.

Bella corrected her with a look.

Sarah and Andi exchanged a glance and started laughing.

"What's so funny?" Duncan looked down at his plate and resumed eating.

"Bella."

Duncan looked her way, and Bella wished she could sink into the floor. She shrugged.

"Bella's funny?"

Ethan narrowed his eyes and looked from Andria to Sarah, to Bella, and finally Duncan. "They sound like the girls at school when someone's sweet on someone else."

"They do, huh?" Duncan grinned around his bite of bread. He leaned back and chewed slowly. "So who's sweet on whom?"

"Well it certainly isn't us," Andria hurried to say.

They both looked over at Bella. She could feel her face redden as everyone at the table stared at her.

"Well it certainly isn't me, either. I'm not sweet on anyone. Though you *are* rather cute, Ethan." She nudged him with her arm.

Ethan turned bright red and fled the table. "Ain't no girl gonna get a hold on me, I don't care how old she is."

"I think he just called you old, Bella." Sarah laughed.

"Yes, I think he has a bit of work set before him when it comes to dealing with females," Duncan agreed. He wiped his mouth with a cloth. "Ladies, that was one fine meal."

"I wish I could take credit." Bella grinned. "I'm more used to cookin' up the likes of rabbit or fish or venison over an open fire."

"That sounds nice, too," Duncan said. "I hope to get a chance to sample some of your cooking someday soon."

"Really?"

"Why not?"

"You seem so civilized. I didn't figure you for the type to like wild game."

"I haven't always lived in town. I've spent my fair share of time riding around in these hills. I told you that before."

"I guess you did, but it's hard to imagine that." Bella smiled. This was a side of Duncan she hadn't expected to see. She'd love to ride the trails in the hills with Duncan's strong protective presence by her side. Andria's and Sarah's giggles brought her out of the daydream. She'd been twirling a strand of hair around her finger while staring at Duncan like he was her own special Christmas gift. Mortified, she jumped to her feet and started gathering plates.

Duncan, looking flustered, stood and did the same. Their hands connected when they both reached for the same mug and both hurriedly let go. The ceramic mug shattered on the hardwood floor at their feet.

"Don't move. I'll get the broom." Duncan moved across the room with long strides.

Andria's and Sarah's gazes went back and forth from one to the other, their expressions amused.

"You two should go help Ethan in the barn. We need to get the animals settled before nightfall."

"Of course." Andi drew out the words. "You two want to be alone."

"Andria!" Bella gasped. "Go!"

Bella walked over to the front window. Now it sounded like she *did* want to be alone with him! What was her sister thinking? Bella. . .*alone* with Duncan? The last thing Bella wanted was to be alone with him. He had her emotions going in all directions and her thoughts all topsy-turvy. The last thing she wanted was to be alone with the man who had her thinking silly thoughts and making a fool of herself. "I meant you two should go along with Duncan to help Ethan in the barn. You'll need to take some blankets. The men will have to bed down out there. I can get the kitchen in order on my own."

Duncan's touch on her shoulder froze her in place. "They're long gone, Bella."

She spun around. He was right. Her sister and friend were nowhere in sight. "They didn't waste any time gettin' out of here."

He chuckled. "No, they didn't."

"Well as I was sayin', you might as well head on out to help them. I'm sure they have no clue what needs to be done out there, and you seem to have some experience that might help them."

"Bella."

She stopped, halfway to the long board that served as a counter. "Yes?" Her voice shook.

"Am I making you nervous?"

"You are right now."

"I don't want you feeling uncomfortable around me."

"I'll try not to, then."

"You didn't finish your meal. Come over here." He gently took her arm and led her back to her seat at the table. "Sit down and eat. The chores will be waiting when we get to them." He glanced around with twinkling eyes. "Just as they have been for the past few years."

"True."

He sat down across from her, making her feel as nervous as she'd been at the diner.

She pushed the food around on her plate. "I can't eat with you sittin' there starin' at me."

"Why not?"

"I just can't." She took a sip of water. "You unnerve me."

His voice took on a teasing tone. "Is it because you find me handsome?"

The water caught in her throat, and she choked. "I never said that!"

"You kind of did."

"I did not!"

"When your sister was talking earlier?"

"I corrected them. I told them to stop."

"Yet they didn't. They asked what you thought. . . ."

"And I didn't answer."

"You didn't deny it."

"When?"

"When the girls were discussing my finer points just after they brought in the livestock."

"That was their conversation, not mine. If you'll think back, you should have heard me chastisin' them, tellin' them they shouldn't be talkin' about you that way."

"Why? I'm still a man. I appreciate the compliments."

Bella pushed her chair back so fast it tipped over. She'd never felt so uncomfortable around a person in all her life.

"I need to do the dishes."

"Bella." His voice was gentle. "I'm sorry for causing you discomfort. I'll stop."

"It's just that. . .I'm not sure how you make me feel," Bella blustered. "Yes, I do. You—you make me feel flustered. And—and inept. And—and—" She put a hand to her hair, and her shoulders sagged. "And like a complete mess."

"If that's the case, you're the prettiest mess I've ever seen."

She whipped her head up to stare at him. Was the man blind? She wore men's trousers, and her unruly hair was pulled back in a braid. Stray strands tickled her face where they'd fallen out of place. She'd slept on the ground the night before and hadn't had time to freshen up. Yet there he sat, saying such ridiculous things.

She didn't know what to say. No one had ever called her pretty before. Duncan was ruining everything. She'd never be able to be content in her old life now that she'd met him. Though she'd already decided to leave behind their outlawin' ways, she'd been content with the thought of living alone at the homestead with just Andi for company. But now that she'd had a taste of Duncan's sweet compliments, she'd always feel something was missing after he left. She promptly burst into tears at the thought.

Duncan jumped to his feet. "What did I say?" He looked perplexed.

"You just had to get all nice and complimentary, didn't you?" she sobbed. "Now I'm the one who has to live with that."

"But isn't that a good thing? I meant everything I said." He started to reach for her then stopped and let his hands drop to his side. He looked bewildered. "Why is that a bad thing?"

"I can't explain it. I told you, it's hard to put into words. Look, I know it's a part of your profession to say such nice things to the people you meet, and you're supposed to be nice and make people happy, but you really ought to be more careful about who you say them to. Some people might, um, take them to heart and make more of the words than is meant."

"If I said something out of line, I apologize. I never use my words lightly. I always mean what I say. And I'm not in the habit of giving compliments to pretty women. I haven't been a preacher for very long, only a few years, but I know to be careful in my actions toward women. I didn't mean to offend, but something about you catches me unaware. I'm in uncharted waters here, too." He glanced around the room. She figured he was either searching for the fastest way out or for a weapon to use against her if she went batty on him again.

"Really?"

"Really."

"But you seem so confident and always in control."

"Then I do a good job hiding my true feelings, which isn't a good thing. I'll have to work on that some more. I want to be approachable to my parishioners and everyone else around me."

"So you meant the things you said to me?"

"Of course I did." His handsome face tightened with concern. "Why would you think otherwise?"

"I don't know, but you shouldn't say things like that."

He looked hurt, but he nodded. "I think I understand. There's someone else, isn't there?"

"Someone else?"

"Someone else courting you. You have a beau that comes calling, and I've overstepped my position. Is that correct? If so, please forgive me."

"That's not it at all! It's the very opposite of the truth."

"There is no beau?"

"No. I've not even had the chance to ever have one. I

wouldn't know what to do with a beau."

His mouth quirked up into a grin. "I'd be more than happy to instruct you on the subject."

"*You're a pastor,*" she whispered.

Duncan glanced around. "There's no one else here. Why are you whispering?"

"I don't want the others to hear. I don't want to be a part of anythin' that could be interpreted as sordid and make you lose your upright standin' in town."

"I promise you my intentions are nothing but honorable. We're well chaperoned here, and I'll make sure to keep my distance so as not to disturb your delicate sensibilities as to what a preacher can and can't do." He leaned close, and she could feel his breath against her cheek. "But I will have you know that something about you calls to my heart, and I intend to find out what it is. I'm not going to abandon you. I might have to leave soon, but if and when I do, you can rest assured that I will be coming back."

With that, he disappeared out the back door and into the afternoon sun.

Bella bustled around the kitchen, cleaning up the dinner dishes, then slamming pots and pans into the wash water so she could clean them for later meals. The man had some nerve.

"*I'm still a man.*"

As if Bella hadn't noticed that fact.

twelve

With Andria and Sarah's help, Bella dug in to finish cleaning the main areas of the cabin. They spent the better part of the day hauling out junk and sorting through their parents' belongings.

Bella stripped the dingy, rotting curtains from the windows and threw them into the fire pit outside. She remembered back to when the fabric was new and her mother had been so excited to put up such bright, cheery fabric. She'd sewn the curtains herself. Bella's father hadn't always had the hard edge to him that he'd had in his later years. He'd bought the fabric as a surprise for Bella's mother on a Christmas long ago.

Sarah gave the windows a good scrubbing, and they sparkled like new. Even now, with the late afternoon sun slanting through the windows, the room was brighter than it had been when they'd arrived earlier in the day.

Andria stayed busy with scrubbing down every surface in the room. Bella washed the pots and pans and dusted the few collectibles their mother had accumulated through the years.

They worked together to remove the linens from the beds and wash them in the tub that Duncan had dragged over near the back door. He filled the tub with water from the hand pump, and Bella added hot water she'd warmed on the stove.

Duncan grinned at their enthusiasm as they dipped the dusty linens in the warm water and scrubbed at them with vigor. Bella watched as Duncan hung a length of rope from the corner of the cabin to a large branch on the nearby magnolia. After he was finished, the clean linens were placed on the line to dry. The fresh-smelling sheets swayed back and forth on the line in the gentle wind that blew through the backyard.

"I'm not sleepin' in those fresh sheets with all this dirt and grime on me." Bella looked down at her dusty pants and shirt with dismay. "I'll need a good scrubbin' myself after we've finished all this cleanin'."

Andria nodded her agreement. Sarah, on the other hand, looked as fresh and pretty as she had when she arrived earlier that morning.

The final items to be cleaned were the beds. It took everything all three women had to drag the feather mattresses outside and thrash them with a stick. They thrashed until the dust stopped puffing up into the air.

Duncan exited the barn and shook his head. "Y'all should have hollered for me to come and do the heavy lifting."

Bella studied him as he walked over to survey the fruits of their labor. He stood with hands on hips, his dark hair blowing in the breeze. Bella couldn't help but notice the hard muscles under his white, rolled-up sleeves. He looked like he belonged in the hills, working the land; and at the moment, Bella found it hard to imagine him in town, standing behind a pulpit.

She shook herself out of her musings.

"We managed to get 'em out here just fine," Bella retorted with a grin. "But we'll be more than happy to let you carry the heavy ticks back inside now that we're finished. We don't want to chance draggin' them on the dirty ground after all the hard work we put in gettin' 'em clean, do we, ladies?"

"Certainly not," Sarah agreed.

"I'm sure not startin' over," Andria chimed in.

Duncan heaved the first one on his shoulder and carried it inside like it was nothing. He returned for the others while the women watched with interest. He was right. It would have been much easier to let him carry them out in the first place.

With the bed frames clean and the mattresses in place, they decided to rest for a bit. They sat in a circle around the open chest at the end of Bella's mother's bed. The fresh scent of spring blew through the open doors and windows. Her mother's personal items lay in the trunk before them.

"What are you going to do with all your ma's dresses?" Sarah picked up the pretty pink gingham that lay on top and held it against her chest. The garment flattered her fair appearance. The pink in her work-flushed cheeks accentuated the light blue color of her eyes. The humidity set her hair into blond ringlets. Bella knew she looked a fright when compared to her pretty friend.

"I suppose we should fix them up and wear them." Bella sighed. "We can't exactly run around in men's pants and shirts forever. That is, we can't if we end up stayin' here."

"Oh, I agree." Sarah beamed. "And I do want you to stay."

Bella exchanged a look with Andria. "We want to, but we have to take care of some final business first."

"How long will it take?"

"We aren't sure, but we'll be back as soon as possible."

Sarah's face fell. "Do you have to leave right away?"

"No, I think we'll sit tight for a couple more days at least. We might as well finish puttin' the place to rights before we move back in."

Bella lifted a blue floral dress from the trunk and felt

something hard press against her leg.

"What on earth. . ." She reached into the pocket and pulled out a polished stone. "Momma's prayer stone."

Sarah leaned close. "What's a prayer stone?"

"Momma found this pretty polished stone one day over by the stream, and she put it in her pocket. She said she'd carry it always and would remember to pray for each of her children every time she felt it. It was like a reminder for her to pray for us. I have a feelin' she knew the lot of us would require all the extra prayer she could summon up. Even with that, look how things turned out."

"Why would you say that?" Sarah's brows knit together in confusion. "I don't think y'all turned out so bad."

"Thanks." Bella forced a smile. There was so much Sarah didn't know about them. She and her family simply thought the McLeods had moved away.

Bella turned the smooth stone over and over in her hand. The stone felt cool to her touch. She liked the idea that her mother's hands had last touched the stone. "Andi, do you mind if I keep Momma's stone with me? I'd like to use it in a similar fashion. Maybe Duncan will teach me to pray better and I can pick up where Ma left off."

"I'd like that, Bella. It would feel mighty good to know someone was prayin' for us again and askin' God to watch out for us."

Bella slipped the stone into her pocket. "I'm not sure my prayers will account for much, but I'll surely give it a try."

"Why wouldn't you think your prayers would be heard?" Duncan entered the room as Sarah folded the last dress and placed it next to a stack of aprons that had been draped over the bed frame.

Bella sent him an incredulous look. "You have to ask? Surely you've noticed by now that we aren't the most traditional women in these here parts."

"I've noticed, but God loves you anyhow. He loves you no matter where you are and no matter what you're doing."

Bella didn't understand why and told him so.

"Do you remember hearing the Bible story of the prodigal son?"

"Vaguely."

"The woman at the well?"

"No."

"The Bible is full of stories about people who chose the wrong path and how God later led them back to His fold."

"His fold?"

"God is our shepherd, and we're like His sheep. He cares deeply for each and every one of us. If you stray, He'll come after you."

"Oh, I don't think He has a mind to come after me. Or Andi." She placed a hand on top of Andi's. "Sorry, Andi. But I'm sure that's true."

Andria shrugged, not appearing too surprised with her lot in life.

"But it's not true," Duncan interrupted. "Let me show you some examples."

He picked up their mother's worn Bible and opened it to a passage. He read it aloud and flipped to another. He read passage after passage that told about bad choices and God's redemption of the sinners.

"So all those folks in the Bible were outlaws and God took 'em back into His family and forgave them?"

Duncan laughed. "Yes, although I'm not sure the term 'outlaw' existed way back then."

"Thank you, Duncan. That gives me some things to think

on. I find it interestin' to know that God might still love me, poor dressin' style and all."

"He does love you and don't you ever forget it. He doesn't care about how a person dresses. He only cares about the heart." Duncan headed for the door. "I need to go see what Ethan is up to. I'll be back in a bit."

Bella turned to her sister and her friend. "If y'all don't mind, I think I'll head over to the stream and freshen up. Now that we have the cabin tidy, I feel more like a mess than ever."

"You do look a mess." Andria laughed. "And I'm sure I do, too. Maybe we should try out some more of Momma's dresses."

"I think I'd like that."

Sarah bounced on her chair. "You try them on, and I'll fix 'em up for you tonight when I get home. I can take them in and hem 'em up and make them fit y'all just fine."

Andi's eyes lit up. "You can? No more trippin' on Momma's long skirts?"

"I can do better than that. I'll teach you how to hem, too, so we can get it done faster."

The younger girls waved Bella off and turned to their sewing chores. Bella grabbed up the blue floral print and tossed it over her arm. Even when messy, Sarah looked like a proper lady. Bella suddenly had the urge to look like a lady, too.

❧

Bella stripped out of the ill-fitting, confining pants and shirt and tossed them toward the stream's shore with disgust. The filthy outfit floated on the water in the shallows. Dirt and grime slowly seeped from the fabric and made the water murky.

Only a couple of days earlier Bella had hated the thought of donning a dress. Now she wished she could wear one proper-like. Surely Duncan would appreciate her more if she looked and dressed like Sarah. She shook her head to clear the silly thoughts. Bella had surely lost her mind if she thought Duncan would ever show any interest in her.

She glanced over at the pretty blue dress that lay carefully draped over the branches of a nearby bush. She hoped the dress would make her look more feminine. Stacked up to Sarah, she didn't have a chance. Sarah had a sweet nature about her and she'd grown up in a God-fearing home. Chances were, she was the kind of woman Duncan was looking for—if he was looking for a woman at all.

The bar of lye soap she'd dragged along with her waited for her on the shore. She swam over to it and worked it into a thick lather. She washed the grime from her body, spending extra time on her hair. She felt better already, just by being clean. It was exciting to have a fresh outfit ready. She usually scrubbed her pants and shirt just before bed and hoped they'd be dry before she had to put them back on the next morning.

Bella lay on her back in the water and floated in the stream. Though the stream wasn't very deep—only a few feet in depth at the middle—the pool where she'd bathed was deep enough to allow her to float above the water-polished stones that lined the bottom.

She thought about the stories Duncan had read to her. She'd never felt worthy of being a good person, not with the family she'd been born into. But apparently God didn't discriminate according to such things. And her mother had loved the Lord dearly, that should count for something. Bella had only focused on her father's and brothers' choices and habits in the past couple of years, but maybe she should put more weight on her mother's love of the Lord.

If what Duncan said was true, it was possible for Bella to have a relationship with God. Bella's whole life would be changed for the better. She wouldn't have to watch her back anymore. She wouldn't have to wonder if and when and where they'd be caught and taken into custody for their deeds. Her life would be redeemed, and she could turn her back on her outlawin' ways.

Because she and Andria weren't ever willing outlaws, Bella didn't think God would hold their actions against them. She figured He'd just want them to turn away from their former actions and change their ways, like the men and women Duncan had told them about. Bella would be more than happy to do just that. Of course she'd confess everything to Sheriff Andrew just to be sure. If he had a mind to punish them, she'd face whatever charges their sins brought her way.

Her mother would be so happy to know that Bella was considering such a thing. For once she'd feel her prayers had been recognized. Bella suddenly remembered her mother's prayer stone and sat up. She frantically glanced around for the pants she'd left drifting in the stream. How could she have been so careless? She'd just taken possession of the stone, and now she'd possibly lost it.

For a long moment she didn't see the pants. She worried they'd washed downstream. She finally located them in some heavy overgrowth near the shore. She tugged them out of their resting spot and dug her hand into the pocket. She breathed a sigh of relief as her hand closed around the hard stone. She kissed the wet object and waded over to tuck it securely into the pocket of the dress. She'd be more careful with the treasure in the future. Though her own heart was well on its way to being redeemed, she still had work to do when it came to her sister's and brothers' well-being.

thirteen

Two days later, Bella, Andria, and Sarah stood and looked over the transformed homestead.

Pride like Bella had never felt before seeped through her being. The work was much harder than she'd first expected. "Sarah, without you, we'd still be standin' here starin' at a filthy cabin. Thank you for comin' and helpin'."

"That's what friends and neighbors do." Sarah grasped Andi's hand and swung her around in circles. "I so want you both to come home."

Bella watched with mixed feelings. Her outlaw sister looked so normal spinning around and laughing with her childhood friend. But she'd missed out on so many other experiences like this. This should have been Andi's life, not the outlaw one their brothers had forced them into. She was more determined than ever to right the wrongs and get Andria back where she belonged.

Sarah headed over to the clothesline to take down the newly tailored dresses.

Bella took advantage of the moment and pulled Andria aside. "I've been thinkin'. We have to turn in the gold."

"What?" Andria's face fell. "I thought we were going to use it for our fresh start. I don't want to go back to our outlawin' ways. Bella, please reconsider."

"We aren't goin' back to our former ways, Andi. But I want us to have a fresh start. If we take gold that isn't ours to start out with, we're as good as stealin' it from whoever it belongs to."

"I hadn't thought of it that way."

"Neither had I until I started listenin' to Duncan and readin' Momma's Bible these past couple of days." She motioned around them. "Look at what we have here. We have everything we need. We need to trust God to provide anything else we might need."

Andria looked doubtful. "You really think He'll come through for us?"

Bella nodded. "I do. And if you'd start readin' the Good Book, I think you'd agree."

Andi dug into her pocket. "Then I can't keep these gold nuggets I took from the cave. We'll have to return them."

Bella placed them in the pocket of her dress, right next to the prayer stone. "We'll do that as soon as Duncan leaves to take Ethan back to town. We need to talk to Wayne and Charlie, then we need to talk to Sheriff Andrew. We'll tell him about our past, and we'll tell him about the gold."

"What about Duncan?"

"I want to tell him before he leaves. He's been so good to us—he deserves to know the truth."

They headed for the house and met Sarah inside.

The familiar bark of a dog carried through the woods and into the open windows. Bella looked out front, her heart filled with dread. She glanced over at Andi, whose expression mirrored her anxiety. Their worst fears had come true. Wayne had arrived at the cabin.

Sarah glanced from one to the other. "What's wrong?"

"Wayne's here."

"Well, that's a good thing, isn't it? Aren't you excited to see your brother?"

"Not right now."

"Why? Do you think he'll cause a problem?"

"We know he'll cause a problem. Multiple problems."

"Can I do something to help?"

"I don't think so." Bella turned to her. "Or maybe you can. Do me a favor and go out to the barn and try to keep Ethan and Duncan distracted while we talk to Wayne."

"How do I do that?"

"I don't know, think of something! But hurry. Ask about the chickens or the goat."

"I'll be happy to do that." Sarah hurried toward the back door and slipped into the warm afternoon sun.

"I'm sure you are," Bella muttered. She had no doubt her friend had noticed the preacher's good looks. Sarah had admitted as much. What surprised Bella were her feelings of jealousy at the thought.

The barking grew louder.

"Let's go out and meet him. Duncan will be out front before Sarah can stop him if he hears the dog."

They hurried to the path that led to their other homestead. Wayne rode slowly up the trail. He looked harder than ever. His dark hair hadn't been tamed, and his blue eyes were bloodshot.

"Well, lookee at what we have here." His words were slurred, a sure sign that he'd been drinking. "The prodigal sisters have finally come home."

"You're right, Wayne. Now that you mention it, we have come home. Home. Right where we belong." Bella didn't know why she started out with an attack. Wayne wasn't nice at the best of times, but when he'd been drinking he was all but impossible to reason with. Bella and Andria knew to stay clear of him when he was in this condition. Unfortunately, in this case, he couldn't be avoided.

"Home is where I say it is." Wayne leaned forward with his

finger jabbing the air and almost fell from his horse. "And I say home for y'all is at the top of the mountain with me and Charlie."

"Speakin' of, where is Charlie?" Bella asked. Charlie wasn't ever very far from Wayne's side.

"He's workin'."

"Workin' where?"

"Well Bella, maybe if you'd come home like you was supposed to, you'd know where Charlie was and what Charlie's been doin'."

Bella didn't respond. She wouldn't let Wayne goad her.

"Care to tell me why you didn't come home, *Bella*?"

She glanced over her shoulder but didn't see any sign of Duncan, Ethan, or Sarah. "Something came up."

Wayne laughed. "What could possibly come up? I told y'all what to do, and you defied me. You know that's not gonna go unnoticed."

Andria stepped forward, her hands clutched at her side. "We had our reasons, Wayne, and if you'd just listen, you'd appreciate our decision not to come home."

Wayne looked surprised to see Andria stand up to him. "You wanna get in the middle of this, baby sister?"

"I want you to leave Bella alone."

"Cain't do that."

"Why can't you?"

"You know why. We need you both to help out. We cain't have y'all actin' disrespectful. We need to count on you."

"What if we don't want to help out anymore?" Bella stood tall and folded her arms across her chest.

Wayne laughed. "You never were what I'd call willin'. But we cain't do it on our own. We depend on you to distract the targets so we have a chance to act."

Bella jumped back in. "It ain't right what you do, Wayne. There are other ways—better ways—to make a livin'. You and Pa used to run moonshine. Why couldn't you stick to doin' that? Or better yet, do somethin' upstandin' that'll make you proud. Robbin' people—it ain't right at all."

"When did you go and grow a conscience anyway? It didn't use to bother you. What's changed?"

"It's always bothered us. We never wanted to be dragged into your law-defyin' ways. But we've grown up. We know that what you do is wrong. We don't want to be a part of it anymore."

"You ain't gettin' out of it, Bella."

Bella hadn't ever been one to pray, and she wasn't sure she even knew how, but she figured it wouldn't hurt to reach out to God and see what happened. Maybe, just maybe, they'd be able to talk some sense into Wayne and they'd be able to stay on at the homestead right away.

She whispered a prayer for God to help them out.

"Who you talkin' to, Bella? You talkin' to yerself?"

Wayne's interruption caused her to jump.

She wondered if she should explain, but Duncan's welcoming shout from the doorway of the barn made her forget what she wanted to say. Ethan and Sarah were nowhere to be seen.

"Who's the man?" Wayne's whole posture changed. "I *told* you not to show up here with a man."

"No, you told us not to go into town and get ourselves hitched. I've hardly done that." Though the thought of being hitched to Duncan wasn't a totally unpleasant one.

"Then who's the man you dragged home with you?"

"He's the parson in town. He didn't think it right that we were travelin' on our own, and he insisted on escortin' us."

"Did he now. And you couldn't figure out how to say no?"

"We did say no," Andria stated. "He followed us out of town anyway, even though we left the night before we said we'd leave."

Duncan was getting closer.

"You'll get the man away from here, or I'll take care of him for ya. You hear me?"

"We hear you," Bella spat.

"Tell him I'm askin' for directions. Don't let on that I'm your brother. You have two days to send him packin' before I return and take care of him myself."

Duncan walked up and introduced himself. Wayne reached down and shook his hand. "The ladies here were just givin' me directions. I'm afraid I got turned around on a trail somehow."

"That's easy to do up here the way some trails twist and turn," Duncan agreed. "Did they set you straight?"

"I think we came to an understandin', didn't we, darlin'?" He stared down at Bella.

"Sure we did. If you'll just follow the right path, you should be just fine."

Wayne squinted his eyes and looked over at Duncan. "There's a right path for everyone to follow, right, Reverend?"

Duncan studied Bella's brother. "It's true there's only one right path for everyone to follow. It's each person's choice whether he or she follows it or not."

Wayne cackled like the crazy man he was. "Says you."

"Says the Bible." Duncan frowned. "I take it you're not a believer?"

"Not in the least." Wayne spat a stream of tobacco onto the ground near Duncan's boots.

Bella closed her eyes in shame. Duncan didn't know the

uncouth man was her brother, but if she didn't hurry up and get him away from there, he'd figure it out soon enough. And then what would he think of her? She needed to explain things in her own way, in her own time.

Duncan stepped forward and used his body as a shield for Bella and Andria. "You'd best be on your way. I hope you make it safely to your destination."

"Sure ya do." Wayne cackled again. "I'll be sure to let you know."

"No need." Duncan's words left no room for argument. "I think it's best if you head out and don't come back."

"What?" Wayne leaned forward and stared with bleary eyes into Duncan's face. "Preacher man, saver of lost souls, is tellin' me to get lost?"

"You're already lost if you don't abide by God's Word. Only you can change that."

"I thought preachers were supposed to be kind to everyone."

"I don't see that I'm being unkind. I'm merely asking you to leave and not come back. These ladies don't need the likes of you harassing them."

"The likes of me? Maybe they don't want the likes of you harassin' them." Wayne glared at his sisters. "What do you say, ladies? You want him or me?"

"Listen. We gave you the directions you asked for. The sun's gettin' low in the sky. You'd best be goin' on, or you'll get lost for sure." Bella wished her brother would just leave. Her stomach was in knots. Once he decided to let go with his cover, he wouldn't bat an eye at hurting Duncan, and at the moment Duncan was unarmed. They all were.

She should have warned him about Wayne. At least then he'd have had his rifle at the ready. If anything happened to him, his fate would rest on her conscience. And if Wayne went on a rampage, how would she keep Wayne from discovering Sarah and Ethan in the barn? She hoped Sarah had cleared the area when Duncan headed their way. Bella knew Sarah would take Ethan back to the safety of Sarah's home if she needed to. They owed her an explanation, too.

Wayne debated for a moment, and much to Bella's relief, he turned his horse to leave. They watched as he rode silently into the woods. Jake, their dog, stood indecisively at the edge of the trees. Wayne called him, and with one last backward glance, the dog ran off to join his master.

Duncan turned to Bella. "You should have summoned me as soon as that man rode up. This is exactly why it isn't safe for you and your sister to remain here alone."

Bella continued to stare into the trees. "I didn't know what to expect. I didn't want to bother you unnecessarily."

"That's why I'm here, Bella! I want to be here for you. I want you to call me if you need me."

Andria backed away a few yards then turned and headed for the barn.

"You've only just met us. You're only here for a short while. I'm not sure why you feel compelled to help us out, Duncan, but you can't watch over us forever. And when you do leave, we'll be on our own again, dealin' with situations just like this every time our brothers are away on business." Bella looked hard into his eyes. "Who are we gonna summon then, Duncan?"

"That's my point, Bella. Why don't you consider coming back to town with Ethan and me? I can find you a place to stay. I can help you find work. I can't explain why I'm drawn to you, but I am. I want to know you're safe. Andrew sent me up here, but my heart is telling me to stay. When I leave, I want you to come with me."

"We can't do that."

"Why not?"

"We have a life up here. We don't belong in town." Bella paced a few feet away. "I'll not make the same mistake again. Does that make you feel better? I'll keep my rifle at arm's reach. Havin' you here has given me a false sense of security. I let down my guard, that's all. It won't happen again."

"That doesn't make me feel any better." Duncan towered over her, hands on hips. His brown eyes glared down at her. "I don't understand this any more than you do, but I know we were brought together for a purpose and I intend to wait and see what that purpose is."

"You don't even know me, Duncan. For all you know, I could be the worst thing to happen to you as far as your position as preacher goes. You need to leave. You need to go back to your people. You need to get Ethan home to his family."

"I'm not leaving. Not yet anyway. I have a few more days before Ethan's parents return. If you won't come with me, I'll stay here and pray I have some answers before I have to leave."

"Nothin' I can say will make you leave sooner?"

"No. I feel God wants me to stay. I don't want to offend you or cause you any concern, Bella, but I need to follow through on what God has placed on my heart."

Bella panicked. Wayne didn't fool around when it came to this sort of threat. She'd prayed for God to intervene, and Duncan had come to help them. Could he really be sent by God to watch out for them? Was it possible that he was the answer to their problems and that somehow God would use him to get them away from Wayne?

She said another prayer and asked God to make it clear if so. A small seed of hope started to bloom in her heart. Maybe, just maybe, God did care, and He'd help them in this time of need.

fourteen

Bella woke early the next morning and decided to enjoy the view of the sunrise from the cabin's porch. She dressed quietly and wrapped a blanket around her shoulders to ward off the early morning chill. She slipped outside and settled into her mother's old wooden rocking chair. The side porch had the best view of the mountains. It was Bella's favorite place to sit and think.

As she watched, the early morning sun began to rise up over the trees. The sky turned from dark blue, to light blue, then lavender, pink, and finally orange as it worked its way higher in the sky. The birds welcomed the morning by calling back and forth to each other from the treetops.

The cacophony of birdsong was so loud, it didn't surprise her to see Duncan walk out of the barn. He headed over to the newly primed pump and shaved before splashing fresh water on his face and hair. He spotted Bella on the porch and headed her way.

She greeted him with a smile. "Beautiful mornin' today."

"Aren't all mornings beautiful up here?" He climbed the steps two at a time and walked up beside her to lean against the rail. He watched quietly for a few moments as the sun climbed higher in the sky. "Nothing I've seen beats the beauty in these hills."

His tender glance swept over her, and for a moment Bella had the strangest sensation that his words described more than just the scenery. Duncan was so breathtakingly handsome that Bella had a hard time keeping her mind on their conversation. She had to agree with his observation when it came to the beauty that surrounded them. The comment suited him as well. With his dark hair still damp from the hand pump and the fresh scent of shaving soap wafting her way in the gentle morning breeze, it was all she could do to speak.

She finally found her tongue. "I s'pose you're right. It is mighty pleasant to sit out here and enjoy the view." So much for witty conversation. Bella smiled. At least she was being civil. She hadn't been all that nice when they'd first met. She forced her eyes away from him and concentrated on studying the low-lying, mist-covered valleys. It had been a long time since she'd taken time to appreciate the beauty of their surroundings.

She wasn't used to letting down her guard. Duncan's presence on the porch and his nearness made Bella feel safe and secure. She wasn't used to either sensation. She wondered how empty the porch would feel once he was gone. Bella was afraid the entire homestead—maybe even the whole mountain—would feel the loss of his presence.

She kept her eyes averted as she spoke, afraid her emotions would be written on her face. "You don't sound much like a city boy at the moment. What part of the mountain are you from? You seem familiar with the area."

"I grew up right here in these hills." He turned to her with a smile. He pointed to the next mountain over. "I was born and raised on that mountain. And I'm wondering at the moment what I was thinking when I decided to settle and preach in town." He sighed and shook his head. "Sometimes you don't know something's missing until it's staring you in the face."

Bella knew what he was saying. She felt the same way about the homestead, but even more so, she felt that way about Duncan. "It seems to me you were in town because God told you to settle down there."

"I guess He did, but I think now He might be calling me in a new direction."

"Just like that?" Bella wished she had such clear direction from God.

"Just like that." Duncan rested his elbows on the rail and looked over at her.

Bella shifted in her chair so she could see him better. "And what would that new direction be?"

"I'm not sure, but I think maybe He's calling me back into the hills."

"You'd leave your church?" Bella's heart skipped a beat at the thought of Duncan living nearby. She didn't want her selfish thoughts to interfere with what God had for Duncan, but if what he said was God's will, she sure hoped he took God up on the offer. "What would you be doin' way up here?"

"Same thing I did down there." He grinned. "I'd still preach, I'd just preach to a new group of faces."

Bella frowned. "I'm not so sure you'd have a good reception. Folks up here tend to hold a person at arm's length when it comes to outsiders. My momma learned that the hard way, and she lived here most of her life."

"Good thing I'm not an outsider then, hmm?" He nudged her with his shoulder. Her arm tingled from the contact.

"You'll have to convince them of that first."

"I'm sure we can find middle ground after we start comparing kin. My family goes way back in these hills."

"Mine, too. Or at least they did." But now most of Bella's family was gone, and she had only her wild brothers and

Andria as far as family went. "Why would you want to settle way out here anyway? It has to be easier in town."

"Easy isn't always best."

"I s'pose not."

"I want to ask you something. That rider, the one who dropped by yesterday afternoon. . ."

A high-pitched shriek just beyond the trees had Duncan standing upright. He motioned for Bella to stay put, snagged his rifle from its perch on the steps, and hurried over to see what had caused the noise. Bella slipped inside and reached for her own rifle. She reached the porch in time to see Duncan assisting Sarah from the path. He'd slung his rifle over his shoulder, and Sarah leaned against him for support.

"She twisted her ankle."

"Oh, Sarah! I'm so sorry." Bella turned the rocking chair so Sarah would have easy access when she got to the porch. "Bring her up here. I'll get somethin' for her sore ankle to rest on."

Bella hurried inside and woke Andria. Andria got up to dress then headed to the well to fetch some cool water for a compress.

When Bella stepped back outside, Duncan had situated Sarah in the chair.

"I feel so clumsy." Sarah fought back tears. She drew in a breath and exhaled. "One minute I was hurryin' over here so I wouldn't miss a moment of our day together, the next I was trippin' on an arched tree root. My foot stayed stuck as the rest of me went down."

Bella cringed. "That must have hurt somethin' awful."

"It did and still does."

"Andria went for cool water."

"Thank you." Sarah tried to gather herself. "I have no idea

how I'll get back home."

"I'll make sure you get there." Duncan looked relieved to have something he could do. "I'll put you on my horse and lead you home that way."

"That would be wonderful." Sarah's face lit up. "Ma's wanted to meet you and Ethan, and she's wanted to see Andria and Belle ever since I told her y'all were here. Why don't you come along and we can make a day of it. Ma would love to make a big dinner and catch up while you're there. Ethan would have fun playing with my brothers."

Bella hesitated then realized this gave her the perfect opportunity to slip up to the caves and check out Andria's golden treasure. "I'd love to, but I have some things I need to do today."

Sarah's enthusiasm waned.

Bella felt bad. "Andria and Ethan can still go along with Duncan. I'll be the only one missin'. I'll finish up what I need to do here, and I'll have a hot supper waitin' when everyone gets home."

Duncan was already shaking his head. "I won't want to leave you on your own here. What if that drifter returns?"

"I can handle the likes of him. I doubt he'll return this soon, but if he does, I'll make sure I have my rifle by my side."

"I don't know. I still don't feel right about leaving you on your own."

"We'll be on our own anyway once you leave to take Ethan home." She stared up at Duncan. "If you're serious about movin' up here and makin' a fresh start, it'll do you good to visit with Sarah's family. They have a lot of standin' and respect in these parts. Their word and encouragement will go a long way in helpin' you start out."

"When you put it that way, it does sound like a good opportunity." Duncan looked impressed. "Thank you, Bella. I'll do just that."

"Glad I could help y'all out," Sarah teased from her perch on the chair.

"I'd rather you not have hurt your ankle, but it does give Duncan a good opportunity to meet some people." Bella laid her hand on Sarah's shoulder. "Tell your ma I'll come to visit soon."

"I'll go round up Ethan and the horse, and we'll be on our way. That ankle is only going to hurt worse as the day goes on. I'd like to get you settled at home before it gets too bad." Duncan leaped from the porch and headed for the barn.

Sarah turned her attention on Bella. "You're sure you can't come along? Can't your chores wait?"

"Not really." Bella didn't elaborate. "But my stayin' here will speed along the process so we can move back here permanently."

"Then get whatever it is that needs doin' done!"

Bella laughed. "I'll get on it as soon as y'all head out."

Andria returned from the well, and Bella slipped inside to get an old rag. They dipped the rag in the cool water and placed the compress on the rapidly swelling ankle. Bella sent Andria inside to gather her things. Duncan and Ethan arrived with Blaze and led him over to the porch.

Duncan left Sarah and Ethan with Andria and motioned for Bella to step around the corner of the cabin. He reached for her hand. "I don't feel right about leaving you here alone. Why don't you join us? I can help with whatever it is that you need to do after we return."

"It's not something you can help me with," Bella hedged. "I need some time alone. I'll be careful, and I promise I'll keep my rifle close at hand."

Duncan was too much of a gentleman to argue, but Bella could tell he wasn't happy about the arrangement.

"I want to talk to you tonight." Bella figured that evening would be as good a time as any to tell him about her family and past. "There are some things about my family and my life that I want to share with you."

"I look forward to my return, then. I want to know you better. We'll stick around Sarah's family's place until after dinner, but we won't stay all day. I'll make our excuses and head back as soon as I can." He leaned forward and kissed Bella on her forehead.

She wondered what it would be like to have him press his lips against her own.

"Until later, then." He moved away and led her toward the others.

Bella knew he'd be later than he thought. When Sarah's family had a visitor head their way, they had a way of making the event a day-long celebration. She nodded, knowing she had to make haste if she wanted to get all the way up to the caves and back before he returned.

❧

As soon as they were gone, Bella headed for the barn. She readied her horse and swung up onto the saddle. The skirt of her long dress hindered her movements, and she wondered if she should change into her pants and shirt. She decided that would be best. She dropped down and walked to the cabin to change. As she neared, she saw that Wayne leaned against the cabin's back door.

Her airway closed off, and she found it hard to breathe. "Wayne."

This couldn't be good. She glanced back at the trail where

she'd last seen Duncan. She willed him to come back. She knew he wouldn't—all his attention would now be focused on Sarah and her painful ankle. And even if he did come back, the resulting battle wouldn't be good.

"Looks like you're in a hurry to get somewhere, little sister."

"Not really. I was just headin' out for a short ride. I haven't taken Steadfast on a trail for a few days and figured he'd be ready to run around a bit."

She wondered if she had time to jump back up on the horse and get away before Wayne could stop her.

He guessed her thoughts and leaped from the porch, landing by her side. He grabbed her by the arm. "Don't lie to me. I always know when you're lyin'. And don't be thinkin' you can get away."

She jerked her arm from his grasp. "What do you want with me, Wayne? You said we had a couple of days. I said I'd get rid of the preacher, but I need more time."

"I have a better idea." He grinned at her, his eyes cold. "What do you think about comin' with me now? The preacher will leave soon enough if you're out of the picture."

"My presence doesn't have anything to do with his visit here. I told you, he wanted to make sure Andi and I made it safely back to the cabin."

"Seems to me you made it back, and he's still lingerin' around."

"He's thinkin' 'bout movin' back to the hills to preach. That's the only thing holdin' him here. He's tryin' to meet some of the locals to see if they'd be receptive of his preachin'."

"Then it won't matter if you come with me."

"It'll matter to Andria. She'll be frantic."

"Go inside and write her a note. And while you're at it, change out of that ridiculous dress. You won't be of any use to me if you're wearing that." Bella's blood ran cold. The only way for her to "be of use" to Wayne was to help him rob innocent travelers. She couldn't do it again. She wouldn't. She had to refuse. "No."

Wayne stared her down, his eyes crazed. "No, what? No you won't change? Or no you won't write Andi a note?"

"No to all of it." Bella stood her ground. "I won't have a part in hurtin' innocent people anymore. I won't be an accomplice to your robberies. If you insist on breakin' the law, find another way to do it that doesn't involve Andria or me. We're stayin' put."

Wayne was in her face and had her arm in his viselike grip before she could take a step backward. "You'll do this last run and then you can take your sorry attitude and go wherever you want. But I promise you that after your part in this, you won't be able to point a finger of blame toward anyone but yourself."

"I won't hurt innocent people."

"You'll do what I tell you to do."

Bella would die first. Tears blurred her vision. And she likely would. She might never see Duncan or Andria again after today. Her last words to Duncan had upset him. He'd blame himself if anything happened to her.

"I'll write that note." She shoved past Wayne and headed for the porch, but he followed her up the stairs. He leaned in the doorway and watched as she wrote. "Tell her what you told me. You wanted to take Steadfast for a ride."

"She'll still be frantic if I don't return in time."

"In time for what?"

"I promised I'd make them supper."

"Aw, isn't that sweet of you? I can't guarantee you'll be back for supper, but we'll see what we can do." His sarcasm made it clear he didn't care if he had her home on time or not. And since he preferred to do the robbing in the early morning hours, she knew she wouldn't be back before dark.

Bella chose her words for the note carefully. She had a feeling Wayne wouldn't bring her back at all. She wanted Andria to get safely away from the area, and she wanted to leave a message so Duncan would gather a posse.

In the end she knew she had no choice but to do as Wayne instructed. He'd tear the note up if she defied him, and Andi wouldn't ever know what happened to her. She finished up and stepped away from the table. "I need privacy if I'm to change my clothes."

"I'll be right outside, but I can see the note through the window. If you tamper with it, I'll be inside before you can finish it off. You hear?"

"Loud and clear."

Bella moved to the far corner of the room and hurried to change into her riding clothes. At least she wouldn't be hindered by long skirts if she had a chance to get away. Dresses certainly had their downside.

Wayne was getting restless. She could hear him pacing the porch. He called for her to hurry up. She pulled the prayer stone and the three gold nuggets from the dress pocket and walked over to the table. Wayne straightened his posture, daring her to defy him. She held the stone and nuggets carefully in the palm of her hand so he couldn't see them and raised her fingers to her lips. She glared at Wayne as she pretended to kiss her fingertips and laid her fingers on the note.

Wayne glared but didn't seem to notice as she laid the

small pile of stones on the center of the paper. She walked toward the door, using her body to shield the note from sight. Wayne was none the wiser that she'd left behind a clue. She only hoped Andria and Duncan would figure out what the clue meant.

fifteen

Duncan whistled a tune as he led Blaze toward the clearing at the end of the trail. The clearing led him to Bella. The day had been long, and he couldn't wait to get back to her cabin. Though the trip had been a success as far as supporters for a new church went, Duncan couldn't shake the sense of apprehension that had been with him ever since he'd left Bella behind. A few more yards and he'd see the welcoming smoke coiling from Bella's chimney. This late in the evening, she should have supper preparations well under way.

With most of the hard work behind them, he'd enjoy sitting at the table with the group as they told Bella about their day. He wanted to hear what Bella had been up to also. He had a feeling she was on the verge of sharing something important with him. Maybe she finally trusted him enough to share about her brothers. That would sure make things easier for him in the future. He'd be able to open up to her about Andrew's concerns and the need for a posse. He wanted Andria and Bella far away from their brothers when the posse took them in.

Everything was falling in place, and he had a feeling God was getting ready to do some special work in both him and Bella and with the nearby homesteaders. He whistled louder, reflecting his good mood.

Andria laughed from her place on Blaze's back. "Somebody sure is in a cheerful mood this evenin'! If I didn't know better, I'd think you were excited to get back home to my sister."

Home. Duncan would be proud to call the place home. The barn was coming along nicely. He and Ethan had cleaned the stalls and secured the outer doors. They'd fixed a few loose boards in the loft and were ready to fill it with fresh hay. He'd leave that for another time since he didn't know when Bella would be back or when she'd settle there for good.

"If you mean that I'm excited to get back and see that she's okay, then yes, I'm excited to get back to your sister."

"Um-hmm." Andria leaned forward, almost dislodging a worn-out Ethan from his spot behind her. "Are you sure there isn't more to it than that?"

"More to. . ." Duncan choked. "What are you trying to say?"

"It just seems to me that you're sort of protective of my sister. And trust me, Bella doesn't need any protectin'. We've been on our own for a while now, and she's managed to keep us both safe just fine. We've been through a lot."

"I do feel protective—of you both. For whatever reason, God has placed me in a position that allows me to watch over you. Then Ethan showed up, and now he's in my care, too, until I can turn him back over to his father. I think it's all part of God's plan to get me up here in the hills where I can make my time more worthwhile. If I can keep you and your sister safe in the process, I'm happy to oblige."

Andria gave him a skeptical look. Duncan ignored her. He wasn't sure what his feelings were when it came to Bella. She was special to him, but she was possibly an outlaw and he was a preacher. The two didn't mix. She was searching, but until he knew she'd found God, he couldn't move forward with his feelings.

"Seems you'd be happy to oblige in other things, too."

"Andria."

"Sorry, but it's true. I see the way you look at her. My sister doesn't know it, but she needs someone like you."

"I thought she could take care of herself."

"She can, but that doesn't mean she should have to."

"I agree." He frowned as they entered the clearing and he didn't see the expected smoke curling from the chimney. "We'll have to wait and see what happens. In the meantime, why isn't she inside waiting for us?"

Andria's gaze was focused on the dark windows. Worry pinched her features. "Somethin' ain't right."

Duncan handed the reins up to Andria and headed for the house at a run. Andi turned the horse toward the stable.

She called out from the barn doors. "Steadfast is missin'. He ain't in the barn."

Duncan motioned for her to stay put. Andria rode Blaze into the protective frame of the barn. Ethan clung to her back. As soon as they were out of sight, Duncan pushed open the back door of the cabin. The interior was dark and cool.

He found the matches and lit the lantern. The room was empty, just as he'd expected. His boots made a hollow sound on the wood floor as he walked around the room. "Bella?"

There was no reply. He hadn't expected one. He placed the lantern on the table and headed for the front door. He stepped onto the porch. Nothing looked out of place. The rocking chair still sat near the steps where she'd placed it for Sarah. The blanket that had warmed Bella's shoulders at sunrise lay crumpled on the floor where she'd dropped it when they'd heard Sarah's anguished cry. He picked the blanket up and held it close to his chest.

He yelled her name toward the trees as Andria stepped up behind him.

"Duncan, she's gone. I found a note on the table."

Duncan followed her back inside. Ethan huddled in the opposite doorway, watching them with worried eyes.

Andria pointed. The note was on the far side of a vase of flowers. The arrangement hid the note from sight; he hadn't seen it when he placed the lantern there.

A polished stone and three gold nuggets lay on top of the single page of parchment.

"What does it say?"

"It says she's taking Steadfast for a ride. But she wouldn't have stayed out this long, nor would she have parted with the prayer stone if that was the case. Just like our momma, she said she'd never leave it behind. Since she did, she had to have left it as a sign."

"And the gold nuggets? What do they mean?"

"If I'm guessin' right, it means she's headed to the caves where I found a stolen lot of gold. I think the fact that she left the stone behind means that our brother Wayne has her. She wouldn't leave it otherwise. The carrier of the stone has the obligation to pray for the rest of us. She said she'd carry it with her always and it would remind her to pray for our brothers and me. Maybe she figures the stone won't do us any good now that she's with Wayne, but that it'll do her some good if it's with us. She wants us to pray for her. Duncan, I think the fact that she's left it behind means she's in serious trouble."

⁂

"This puts us in a real hard place, Andria." Duncan paced back and forth across the hardwood floor. "We have Ethan to watch out for. I need to gather a posse. I don't want to leave the two of you here alone. Wayne might return."

Andria nodded.

He thought for a moment. "I think we need to head back

to Sarah's. You and Ethan can stay there."

Sparks shot out from Andria's eyes. "You aren't leavin' me behind! I'm goin' with you."

"I'll do better on my own. If you're with me, I'll be worrying about you every step of the way. Stay at Sarah's and pray for Bella's safe return. Let me concentrate on finding your sister."

"I know what my brothers do, Duncan." Andi stared at him with beseeching eyes. "They lead their victims into the hills and rob them."

Duncan's heart went out to her. She was so young. She looked so guilty at having to tell him about their actions. "Everything's going to be okay, Andria."

"No, it's not. Nothin's gonna be okay." Her voiced choked up with tears. "I know this because Wayne makes Bella and me lead the victims in. We duck out through a small cave that leads to the area while Wayne and Charlie do whatever they do. We hole up here at the cabin, which is why it was in such bad shape. We only get to stay until they come after us."

"So you have no idea what your brothers do after you lead the people in?"

"No." Her voice was choked with tears. "Bella said she thinks they've turned more violent. She felt it deep inside. She said it was like a warnin' and that we had to get out as soon as we could."

She wiped at the tears that coursed down her cheek. "Duncan, she stood up to Wayne. Twice. The first time was the day we left for town. She stood up to him, and he knocked her from her horse. She landed flat on her back. She was bruised all the way up her side and shoulder. She had a huge lump on her head."

Duncan's heart filled with rage. If only he'd pushed them

to tell him what he'd overheard that day.

"Then she did it again the other day when he rode up to the cabin."

"The man asking for directions?"

"Yes, it wasn't really a stranger. It was Wayne. Bella said we weren't helpin' him anymore, and he said we were. He looked crazed, Duncan."

"Why didn't y'all tell me?"

"He threatened to hurt you. And he would have. He had weapons; we didn't. Bella wouldn't put you in that position. He gave us two days to send you on your way."

"I had no idea! What kind of protector am I? I've let you both down."

"You don't know Wayne, Duncan. He's dangerous. And I told you Bella's independent. She can handle herself." Her voice drifted off. "Or she used to be able to, before Wayne changed."

"I can be dangerous, too, Andria. Where's your other brother in all this?"

"I don't really know. Charlie has always been at Wayne's side, but he wasn't there the other day. Wayne said somethin' about Charlie workin' when we asked, but he's never sent him off like that before."

"Then we can assume something has happened to Charlie, too."

"He did try to defend Bella when Wayne hurt her." Her eyes widened. "If Charlie's hurt—or worse—that would explain why Wayne needs Bella. When she said that we were done with helpin' them, Wayne said he wasn't goin' to let her go, and instead he'd be initiatin' her into a higher level of service. She's been readin' Ma's Bible faithfully, and she's learned a lot. She said the other day that she wants us to abide by God's Word. We have to get Bella away from Wayne! She'll die before she hurts another person. And Wayne will be happy to oblige that desire if she crosses him."

Duncan stopped pacing and headed for the door. "We'll take Ethan to Sarah's. Ethan can wait there."

"I don't wanna stay there! I wanna help you find Bella." Ethan's angry voice broke into the conversation. "My pa's posse can take care of the bad guys."

"Your pa's posse?"

"Yeah, the one I told you about when I overheard my pa talkin' in town. They said they was goin' after the McLeod gang."

Andria paled. "That's us."

She backed away from Duncan. "Is that why you're here? Did Sheriff Andrew send you to watch over us so's he could go after our brothers? All this time, you were doin' what you did because you were workin' for the sheriff?" She burst into tears. "I thought I could trust you. I really thought you cared about us."

"I do care about you, Andria. I care about both of you." He wrapped his arms around her stiff body and pulled her into a hug. "Everything's going to be okay. I'm here to protect you and Bella, just as I said. We did realize who you were when you arrived in town, but we were after your brothers. We'd heard that a member of the gang found gold, Alex McLeod, but I never heard mention of a family member by that name. I didn't figure it out until I saw the family Bible."

Andria got control of her emotions and stepped back, her gaze wary. "You found what out when you looked at the Bible?"

"You're Alex, right? There are only four listings in there. Wayne, Charles, Isabella, and Alexandria."

"It's true I found the gold. I already told you that. But we were going to turn it in as soon as we had a chance. I think that's why Bella stayed behind today. She told me we couldn't use the gold to start a new life as we'd originally planned when we went into town. She said she'd learned enough from you to know we had to trust God to provide our way. She wanted to turn the gold over to Sheriff Andrew. I think she stayed behind so she could go up there and check things out."

"That makes sense."

Andria glanced over at the table. "I only took those three nuggets as proof of my discovery."

"Who else knew? Somehow word about the gold made its way back to Sheriff Andrew."

Andria dropped her gaze. "I told Sarah. She sometimes calls me Alex. She said she'd keep it a secret. I figured it was safe to tell her about it since she lived way up here in the hills, but she must have told someone else. I didn't tell her where I'd found it, just that I'd found some gold, and I showed her the three nuggets. For all she knew, that was all I'd found. The story must have grown as it made its way to town."

"Stories have a way of doing that." Duncan sighed. "Let's get going. If the story has somehow reached Wayne, Bella won't be safe once she's led him to the treasure."

"I don't think Wayne knows about the gold, Duncan, but I do think he has plans to get rid of her. He was really upset that she defied him. Somethin' inside him is off. He's drinkin' more than usual, too."

"Drinking too much can certainly change a person. We need to find her."

sixteen

Andria wound her way around the mountain with Duncan following as close as he dared. They wove through the trees with the full moon lighting their path. Animals scurried out of their way, rustling the brush on either side of the trail. The night noises kept Duncan focused.

Ethan hadn't been happy about being left behind, but Duncan refused to take him along. Sarah's parents quickly gathered the boys together for prayer, and Ethan had settled in with them. Duncan knew the boy was in good hands.

Andria sat tall in her seat. Duncan could tell by her posture that she was upset. "We're going to get to Bella, Andi. You lead me to the back side of the escape cave, and I'll go in after her. The posse should already be in the area. We'll find them. We're going to get her back."

She didn't answer for a moment. Her posture remained tense. "He won't act until mornin'."

"Pardon?"

"Wayne. He never strikes in the dark. He'll wait till mornin' light."

"Then we have time to plan."

"Yes."

They rode for two hours before spotting a small campfire in the trees ahead. Duncan urged Blaze to move up beside Andria's horse. "You sit tight and let me ride up and check things out. I don't want to ride into an ambush."

"All right, but it's probably just some cowboys passin'

through and restin' for the night."

Andria had spunk, Duncan had to give her that. She didn't spook easily. "If it's all the same to you, I'd still like to take a closer look before we ride in. It's never a good idea to catch a group like this unawares."

Andria smiled. "We don't usually take the chance to find out. We usually ride away from groups of people out here, not to them."

She and Bella had lived such a different life than him. Even during his own outlaw days he'd made friends along the trail. The McLeod gang was a solitary bunch, which is why they were so hard to catch.

He followed the faint path and cautiously made his way toward the circle of men. He'd acted as deputy enough to recognize Andrew's hat and posture as he neared. He motioned for Andria to join him. Duncan called out to the group before they rode into the encampment.

"Duncan! You're a sight for sore eyes. We're gettin' closer to catchin' the McLeods. As a matter of fact, we might have stumbled upon one of them this afternoon."

His voice drifted off when he registered Andria at Duncan's side.

Duncan motioned to her. "You remember Andria."

Andrew hurried to his feet to help her down from her horse. "Miss McLeod. It's a pleasure to meet you again."

"She knows what's going on." Duncan answered the unspoken question in Andrew's eyes. "Her brother, Wayne, arrived at the homestead yesterday afternoon and threatened Bella. At the time, I didn't know who he was. He told Bella she had two days to get rid of me."

Andria jumped to his defense. "You had no way to know, Duncan. Don't blame yourself."

"This morning Andria and I had to escort an injured neighbor home, and Bella begged off, saying she had things to do." He shook his head. "I should have known she was planning something."

Again, Andria interrupted. "Bella's good, Duncan. If she doesn't want you to know somethin', she makes sure you don't know."

"So I noticed. That doesn't make it any easier to stomach."

He turned back to the posse. "Bella's brother, Wayne, apparently decided to come back a day early. He took Bella with him. Or at least, that's what happened to the best of our knowledge."

Andria explained about the stone and the nuggets of gold. "We think Bella was plannin' to check out the cave with the gold, but Wayne intercepted her before she could get there. He's been actin' mighty funny. And we're worried about our other brother, Charlie. He doesn't usually leave Wayne's side, but he wasn't with him yesterday."

Andrew exchanged an uneasy glance with one of the men. "Maybe you can come over and identify a man we came across yesterday mornin'. He can't talk to us, but we figured him for one of the McLeods."

He led the way over to a small outcropping of rocks. Duncan noticed a still figure lying on top of a bedroll.

Andria hurried over and dropped to her knees. "Charlie!"

The figure didn't move.

"What happened to him?"

"We aren't sure. We found him unconscious at the top of the trail. Looked like he was hit pretty hard on the head and tried to make it to help."

"Is he gonna be all right?" Tears poured down Andria's cheeks.

"We sure hope so. We've tried to keep him comfortable. We don't want to move him too much since we aren't sure about the extent of his injuries. Mason rode for Doc. They should be back anytime. We figured it was Doc ridin' in when you arrived."

He lowered his voice and talked to Duncan as Andria turned her attentions back to Charlie. "We figure we'll keep Doc around until tomorrow afternoon. He can stay with Charlie while we go after Wayne. We might be needin' his services again before the day is out."

Duncan walked over and knelt at Andria's side. "He's resting comfortably. His breathing looks good."

"I've never seen Charlie so quiet."

"He'll be fine. Let me pray for him."

She lowered her head and listened along as he prayed for her older brother. She said a quiet "amen" when he finished up the prayer.

Two men on horseback announced their arrival on the heel of the prayer.

"That's Doc in the black coat," Duncan explained. "He'll take good care of Charlie."

A chill was setting into the night air, and she shivered. Duncan led Andria over to the fire. "We're going to make sure Charlie is okay, and we're going to get Bella safely home. In the meantime, tell us everything you know about Wayne and what he might have planned."

Andria glanced around the circle of tough-looking men. Most women would be too intimidated to speak to such a group, but Andria lifted her chin and began to talk. Duncan felt as proud of her as he would if she were his own sister. He admired her gumption.

"Wayne will wait in a small clearin' in the trees up the hill from the cave trail. The main trail is safer, but lots of folks take the cave trail to save time. Bella and I move out of the trees as soon as we hear travelers approachin'." She took a moment to gather her thoughts. "Every once in a while we run into someone we know. If we do, we have to pretend we're out for a ride. We wait for them to leave, and the process starts all over again."

"So Wayne's attacks are chance, not something he plans in advance?" Andrew leaned forward, focused on every word.

"Right. He sits back and chooses his victims as they pass by."

"So what happens when someone you don't know passes down the trail?"

"Wayne whistles, mimickin' a bird when he wants us to lead someone in. We hesitate near the fork in the path, and when they ride up, we tell them we're tryin' to decide if we want to go along the more populated trail or if we want to take the faster trail through the caves." She shuddered. "Usually they'll encourage us to take the faster trail and will offer to escort us in."

"I take it you've had some bad experiences with that?"

"Many." She closed her eyes. "Most of the men attack us before Wayne and Charlie ever decide to show up. Wayne says he prefers for that to happen. Says it makes it all the sweeter to be able to protect helpless women in need while robbin' the poor fools who fall for our act."

"He put you and Bella at risk for his own gain."

"As often as he could get by with it."

"What did Charlie say?"

"Charlie was our defender. If Wayne waited too long, we could always count on Charlie to come through for us. Even the time one of the men almost had his way with Bella. . ."

She let her voice drift off. She cleared her throat. "Charlie got there in time. He was fightin' mad."

"How long ago did this happen?" Duncan felt his face redden with anger. He prayed he'd be the one to take Wayne down. He didn't think it was the most appropriate prayer he'd ever lifted up to God, but he also figured God understood his anger.

" 'Bout three weeks ago, I s'pose. That's the first time Bella asked Wayne to consider changin' his callin'. Wayne laughed in her face and said he'd never change. Charlie got in Wayne's face and told him he'd best not put either of us in that situation ever again."

"What happened after that? Did Wayne change his ways?"

"Not in a good way. He sent Bella to the homestead to gather up a couple of Momma's dresses for our trip to town. Meanwhile, he used me to lead a group in on my own." Her face pinched. "I hadn't ever had to go in alone. Charlie said he'd watch out for me, and he did. Wayne said I'd best not tell Bella or I'd be sorry. He was so different he scared me. I didn't tell Bella until later. I told her when we went to town."

A look of horror rushed across her face.

"Charlie isn't up there to protect Bella. Wayne will take a sick satisfaction in seeing Bella hurt. If he had anythin' to do with Charlie's beatin'—and I think he did—he'll not hesitate to let Bella get hurt, too."

"Not if I have any say in it." Duncan was well aware of Andrew's questioning look. "I'll ride up there tonight if you tell me where to go. Bella won't be hurt at Wayne's hands."

"It's not Wayne's hands I'm worried about in this case," Andria muttered.

"I know."

Andrew intervened. "If you'll excuse me for interruptin', I'd like to say a few words as sheriff."

Duncan motioned for him to go ahead.

"First of all, we aren't goin' to go rushin' into this all willy-nilly." He stared hard at Duncan. Duncan kept his focus on the fire. "Second of all, Duncan, I have half a mind to keep you back here with Andria, Charlie, Doc, and Doc's assistant when the rest of us ride in."

"You aren't keeping me from rescuing Bella."

"That's what I thought."

Andrew's contemplative expression rubbed Duncan wrong. He knew he needed to get control of his anger and his thoughts, but this was Bella they were talking about. "I'm not sitting out when Bella's in trouble."

"You won't do anyone any good if you ride in there and aren't thinkin' straight. You need to settle down."

"I'll settle down after she's safe. This is *Bella* we're talking about. What if it were your wife or your son?"

"I'd do anything to keep my family safe, Duncan. You know that. But I'd also act within the law as much as possible. I'd think things through so my actions didn't have the wrong result and end up gettin' 'em killed."

Duncan blanched at the thought. There were so many things he wanted to say to Bella. They'd talked enough during the past couple of days that he felt pretty sure she had a good grasp on God. She'd asked Duncan to pray with her several times. And based on his conversations with Andria, he felt pretty sure Bella had given her heart over to the Lord. But there was so much more he wanted to teach her. He wanted to be by her side as she learned to trust and rely on God. He wanted to be by her side as she started her new life on the homestead.

"You've fallen in love with her, Duncan." Andria's eyes lit

up at the thought. "We'll get through this, and then you need to tell her."

Duncan didn't even care that a group of the toughest men in town heard her words. Most of them were hitched anyway and understood what he was going through.

"We'll get them, Duncan," Andrew said. "But you know when we do, Bella will be tried for the crimes right along with her brothers."

Andria gasped.

"I'm sorry, ma'am, but that's the hard truth." Andrew looked Andria in the eye. "I'll do my best to prove that you were both reluctant to participate at the very least. And because you're so willingly workin' with us now, I think we'll be able to keep you and Bella out of trouble."

"Thank you." Her voice was barely a whisper. She looked terrified for a brief moment then quickly pulled herself together and covered up all emotion. "Duncan, maybe you should tell him about Ethan."

"Ethan?" Andrew's eyebrows rose. "What's the boy done now?"

"He followed me up the mountain and didn't show himself until it was too late for me to turn back."

"That can't be right. He's supposed to be with his mother in Atlanta."

"Apparently she got upset with him and left him to stay with you. He rode into town and overheard you mention that you were going with the posse. I was leaving town, and he got the idea to tag along."

"That boy!" Andrew pulled his hat from his head and ran his fingers through his hair in frustration. "Where is he now?"

"He's safely tucked away at Bella's neighbor's house.

They'll take good care of him until we can get back up there and retrieve him."

"Good."

Doc entered the circle and settled down next to Andria. "Your brother should be good as new once he rests a bit. He has a concussion, and he'll have quite a headache before he feels better. Someone hit him hard on the head. It's a miracle he's alive."

"Charlie's always had a hard head."

"Well, in this case his hard head saved his life. I'll stay close and watch him through the night." He patted her hand. "We'll talk more in the mornin'. This old man needs to get his tired bones in bed for now. I'll be up and down checkin' on my patient while y'all sleep."

"You'll have company," Andrew stated. "We'll take turns keepin' watch. I don't expect Wayne to show himself down this way based on what Miss McLeod has told us, but it won't hurt to be prepared just in case."

"I'll go first." Duncan stood up and sent Andrew a look that said he wouldn't take no for an answer.

"I'll spell you in a bit. We have enough men here that we can each take an hour and still be fresh in the mornin'."

"I want to leave at first light." Duncan thought a moment. "No, I think we should leave sooner than first light."

"I'm callin' the shots here, Duncan." Andrew glared. "If you can't abide by that, you'll be locked in handcuffs and left with only a tree for company."

"I'll see you bright and early." Duncan figured he wouldn't sleep a wink. He might as well offer to stand watch all night. But he knew Andrew wouldn't allow it and would likely prove his point with the handcuffs.

Duncan wished he'd never joined up with the posse. While

it was good that Andria would have company and could sit by Charlie's side, Duncan would prefer to be standing at the right end of the trail instead of sitting at the wrong end. If he found a way, he'd sneak off after his watch and settle himself into place.

seventeen

Bella pulled at the ties that bound her wrists and tried to loosen their hold. Instead of loosening, the ropes dug deeper into her skin. Tears of frustration threatened to spill over, but she blinked them back. The last thing she wanted to do was let Wayne know how upset she was.

She glanced over at him. "I haven't had anything to eat."

Wayne glared at her. "What's that matter to me?"

"I won't be much help to you if I pass out from hunger."

She hoped he'd release her from her bonds long enough to eat. If he did, she'd take her chances and try to get away. So far he'd kept his rifle propped against his leg, allowing no opportunity for escape. He'd spent the better part of their time together drinking. If she caught him at the right moment, she could probably escape. Even if he was able to reach his gun and aim before she ducked behind some trees, he wouldn't be too accurate a shot with all the whiskey he'd consumed.

"I'll take my chances. I'm not givin' you any vittles. Stop aggravatin' me."

Bella sank back in despair. She didn't want to help Wayne with his next robbery, even this one last time. He scared her.

"Why won't you tell me where Charlie is?" She tried to find a more comfortable position and winced. The ropes had rubbed her raw in several places, and every time she shifted she reopened a wound. "What have you done with him?"

Wayne spit. "What makes you think I done somethin' to him? Maybe he's just busy."

"He's never been too busy before when it came to helpin' you out. I used to think it was because he was so committed to you and the robberies. But you know what I think now?"

"No, but I'm sure you're gonna tell me." He sounded bored, but his words were beginning to slur. "What do you think, Bella?"

"I think he also told you that he didn't want to be a part of this anymore and you did somethin' to hurt him. That's why you need me so bad. You need money for your next bottle of whiskey, and you don't have any help. Far be it for you to get up and make your own livin' in a legal way." Her voice rose with anger as she stated each word. "You prefer to make us all do your illegal work while you sit all safe and sound hidden up here in the trees."

"I've done my part through the years. And for your information, I can make my own livin' if I want to. But why do that when I can use you?"

"You can't use me. I won't help this time. I already told you that."

"And I already told you that you will help or you'll pay a heavy price."

Bella had already set herself straight with God. She knew the price she'd pay if she refused Wayne. But she'd also pay a price if she went against what God wanted her to do. "I'm willin' to pay that price. I won't help you out, Wayne. Not now. Not ever. You're on your own this time."

"Then you must not know the price I'm askin' of ya, little sister."

"Oh—I think I do. But I won't put my own safety above that of an innocent stranger's."

"Innocent? If I recall properly, some of those *strangers* tried to take liberties with you and Andi. You think that's what upstandin' people do? The men we rob deserve every bit of what they get and then some."

"No, I don't think upstandin' people do things like that, but that still doesn't make what you do right."

"I ain't never said it was right. And I reckon that I don't care."

"Why don't you care? You weren't like this when Momma was alive. Papa wasn't either. Was it her death that set you two off? We lost her, too, you know."

"I haven't ever taken the time to think it out, Bella. We did what we had to do."

"No. You didn't. Papa took care of us just fine. You and Charlie could have looked for honest work. And maybe you should take the time to think about it. You didn't have to become outlaws. You chose to."

"Yep."

"And you dragged the rest of us along with you."

"That we did."

"It wasn't right."

"Agreed."

"Then why'd you do it? I hate when you act like this. I might as well be talkin' to this tall pine tree you tied me to."

"I'm uppin' the ante, Bella. How's that for talk?"

"Uppin' the ante how?" Bella narrowed her eyes.

"I want you to be involved with the entire process. You won't ride off after we corner the victim. You'll stay to help this time."

"I just told you I won't help you anymore. Are you even listenin' to me? I'm not helpin' you lead anyone in. I'm not leavin' anyone alone with you. And I'm not gettin' more involved with the process. I quit. I'm done. And so is Andria."

"See, Bella, that's just the thing. You don't have the

privilege of quittin'. You have to do as I say."

"No I don't."

"Yes you do." Wayne moved close. The stale odor of whiskey mixed in with his unclean body assaulted her senses. "You will do exactly as I say, or you'll regret it."

"I already regret everything I've done for you in the past, Wayne. I won't add more regrets to the list. You'll have to kill me first. I have my life right with God, and you can't intimidate me anymore."

Wayne's face turned purple with rage.

"How dare you defy me!" He slapped her hard on her cheek.

Bella's head snapped back against the tree, and she saw stars. The tears broke free and poured down her face. "I won't do it."

"You'll not only do it, you'll kill the person we rob. How do you like that? You'll never be able to point your self-righteous finger at me. The whole time you're robbin' the person, I'll have my rifle sight trained on the back of your head."

Bella's head ached, and she wished he'd just finish her off then and there. "You said I'd pay a heavy price. I'll pay it now. End this."

He laughed. "What price do you think you'll pay?"

"I s'pose you'll make me pay with my life. I'm ready to do that."

Her mind cried out that she wasn't ready. She wanted to be there for Andria. She wanted to keep her safe. Bella uttered a desperate prayer for the safety of those she loved. She prayed that God would intervene and keep her safe. She'd never been so afraid in her life. She hoped Duncan and Andria had figured out her clues, but she didn't see how they could gather help and arrive in time even if they did. She said a final prayer in the hopes that God would direct Duncan to watch out for Andria if anything happened to Bella.

"I'm not takin' your life, Bella. That wouldn't be nearly as much fun as watchin' your face when I bring Andria into the fold. It's time she became a bigger part of things, too."

"You leave her alone!" Bella fought the ropes that held her, tearing more skin in the process.

Wayne only laughed.

He knew he'd won. She'd do anything to avoid Andria being hurt. Bella felt peace that Duncan would watch out for Andria, but he couldn't watch her every moment and she knew it was only a matter of time before Duncan let his guard down and Wayne went after their sister.

❧

"Wake up, little sister. It's time for us to go." The early morning sun formed a halo around Wayne's head.

Bella squinted as she pushed herself up from the hard-packed earth and tried to see her brother's face. It was hidden in shadow. He towered over her, his rifle in one hand and the horses' reins in the other. "C'mon. I want to get an early start."

Bella shifted around so he could cut through the ropes that bound her hands together. If he noticed the damage they'd done to her wrists, he didn't let on.

The ground shifted away from Bella as she stood. She leaned on the tree for support. Tired, dizzy, hungry. . .she wasn't feeling real confident when it came to pulling off whatever her brother had in mind.

One thing she was sure of—she wouldn't hurt another person. Andria's face came to mind, but Bella pushed it away and focused on praying instead. *Lord, please keep Andi safe. Please be with me in this time of need and help me stop my brother from whatever it is he plans to do. In Jesus' name. . .amen.*

Bella realized that as woozy as she was, she'd be hard-pressed to make a fast escape. That explained Wayne's reluctance to let her have dinner the night before.

"Can I have a bite to eat before we go?"

Wayne stared down at her. "After we finish our day's work."

He half lifted, half pushed Bella up onto her horse. She continued to pray that God would show her the way out. Wayne motioned for her to follow him, and she did as he requested, though she continuously scoured the countryside for any signs of help.

They were just approaching the split in the trail when a huge explosion rocked the air. The horses reared, and Bella fought to keep her hold on the saddle horn. Wayne continued to battle his much larger horse, and Bella took advantage of the opportunity. She urged her horse to run, guiding him in the direction of their escape route. She knew Wayne would be on her heels in an instant, but she felt her only chance would be to lose him on one of the many winding trails.

She and Andi were much more familiar with the area than Wayne, and Bella used that to her advantage. She took some of the lesser-used paths, knowing that Wayne seldom came this way at all. He and Charlie took the faster route home and rode out the way they came in.

Andi and Bella took pride in finding new paths, cutting new trails, and disappearing as soon as they were spotted by any of their victims who happened to ride after them.

She rode hard, her breathing matching the horse's as they ducked through low-lying branches, jumped over stumps or large rocks, and tore through openings in the brush. She could hear Wayne behind her but didn't dare to look back to see how far behind he was.

The passage twisted and turned, and for a brief moment she panicked, knowing nothing but empty trails waited for her on the other side of the mountain. *Lord, please help me get out. I have so much I want to say to Duncan. I want to tell Andi what I've learned about trust. I want her to know You.*

The crashing neared, and Bella bent low on her horse, riding for all she was worth. He was gaining on her. And she had no doubt that when he caught up with her this time, she wouldn't get away again.

Movement to her right caught her off guard. Her horse slowed as a large figure burst from the brush and headed straight for Wayne.

Duncan!

He yelled for her to keep moving, and she did as he requested.

Wayne screamed—whether in terror at being thwarted or anger that someone had bested him, Bella didn't know. She didn't stay around long enough to find out, either. She heard a huge crash in the trees behind her and kept moving forward.

Bella couldn't slow down. She knew she had to make as much progress and get as much distance from Wayne as she could. She began to cry. So many bad things had happened in these hills because of her brothers. Now Charlie was missing and Duncan was alone where she'd left him, fighting a madman. Bella had left Duncan in her dust to fight her battle. And she had no idea where Andria was or how she'd keep her safe.

"Bella!"

Bella was so deep in thought and so filled with terror that

at first she didn't register that her name had been called. Her only thought was to get far away.

"Bella, stop, please!"

Andria's voice started to break through the panic. Bella glanced around.

"I'm over here. Slow down."

Andria rode up beside her and took the reins.

Bella leaned into her arms and cried. "You're safe."

"Of course I am," Andria crooned. "Duncan kept me safe. You're the one we were worried about."

Bella wiped her eyes and reached for her reins. Andi saw her wounds and gasped.

"Wayne did that to you? He tied you up?" Tears of anger and sympathy filled Andi's eyes.

"Duncan went after him alone. We need to get help."

"Sheriff Andrew and some others are already on their way. They took the south trail in case Duncan and I missed you. They'll meet up any minute now."

Bella tried to get her emotions under control. "Charlie wasn't with Wayne. I asked about him, and he wouldn't give me a straight answer. I think Charlie's in trouble."

"Charlie is fine." Andi filled her in. "He's injured, but Doc says he'll be just fine after a few days' rest."

"Wayne hurt him, didn't he?"

"I assume so. He's not conscious right now, but someone roughed him up somethin' awful."

"I want to see him."

"He's just outside the passage. Doc is there with him, and we'll have him look at your wrists. Follow me."

eighteen

Bella waited by Charlie's side until Duncan and the men rode into the encampment. Sheriff Andrew trailed behind with Wayne draped across his horse.

"Is he—?" Andria paled.

"He'll be fine. He put up quite a fight, but we managed to subdue him." He glanced over at Duncan. "We'll head on into town so we can get him in a cell before he wakes. You finish up here and meet up with me later."

Duncan nodded. "I'll gather up Ethan and see you in a bit."

"I want to go with Wayne." Andria glanced over at Bella, her eyes begging for understanding. Bella nodded her approval.

"I'll stay here with Charlie. We'll join you as soon as he's ready to travel."

Andria gave her a spontaneous hug.

"It's okay." Now that the shock had passed, Bella resumed the role of older sister and fell back into her usual habit of reassuring Andi. "We'll all be fine. I'll be right behind you."

One of the men in the posse was giving Bella a strange look. "What about the rest of 'em, Sheriff?"

"What about the rest of who, Clive?" Sheriff Andrew looked annoyed to have been stopped by the member of the posse.

"The rest of the gang. You aren't goin' to leave 'em behind, are you? What if they scatter?"

Sheriff Andrew looked incredulous. "Don't you think Bella would have left already if she'd had a mind to escape?" He shook his head. "And Charlie there can't do much, what with him bein' unconscious and all."

"For all we know Miss McLeod here could be fixin' to run as soon as your back is turned. She knows her siblings are in custody."

"I'll take responsibility for them, Clive. Don't you worry your pretty little head."

Clive glared, and Ben backed him up.

"I have to agree with Clive. These women have been active in the gang from everythin' I've ever heard. We can't go lettin' them walk just because they're of the fairer persuasion."

"Andria is coming to town with you, Clive, and I'll personally make sure Charlie and Bella arrive by nightfall." Duncan spoke from behind Bella. He was close enough that his breath warmed her ears.

Bella waited for the posse to move on and saw a flash of guilt pass through Duncan's eyes when he turned to her.

Her heart sank. "You knew who we were all along, didn't you?"

"I did."

"You're no different than any of the others. You said you were here to protect Andi and me. Instead, you used us to lead you to our brothers."

"That's not true." He reached for her, imploring her to listen, but she only wanted to distance herself from his lies.

"I never expected you to use trickery and deceit in such a way. I thought you were honest and upstandin'. I figured you for the preacher you said you were, not this imposter of a man of the cloth."

"I am honest and upstanding, Bella, or at least I strive to be."

Bella turned her back on him. She didn't want him to see her tears.

"My actions were honorable when it came to protecting you and Andria. I heard you talking in the trees that first day, the day you almost ran us down on the trail. You mentioned your brothers and that one of them had hurt you."

Bella remembered but hadn't realized he'd overheard their conversation about their brothers.

"I didn't know who you were at the time. But when you walked in the diner and introduced yourselves—that's when we knew." He paused. "Your brothers are dangerous men. I wanted to help protect you and help you break free of their hold."

"Why didn't you tell me this from the start?"

Duncan looked amused. "Would you have trusted me?"

"No."

"That's why I didn't tell you. I had to gain your trust."

"By deceiving me?"

"I didn't intentionally deceive you. You just weren't privy to the full situation." He touched her arm, encouraging her to look into his eyes.

Bella obliged.

His deep brown eyes searched her own. "I could say the same about you, ya know."

"That I deceived and tricked you? How do you figure?"

"You didn't let on that you were with the McLeod gang. You insinuated that you lived on the homestead. You knew my heart but didn't let me have any inkling that you were involved with an outlaw gang."

"We do live on a homestead, just not that one. Not very often anyway."

"You didn't tell me Wayne was your brother that day when he first rode in."

"I knew he'd kill you if you figured out who he was and approached him."

"And the fact that you've lived as an outlaw?"

"A reluctant one. I've never wanted to be in the family 'business.' I hate the outlawin' lifestyle."

Duncan sighed and looked out over the trees. The hollow was cool. Bella noticed that the birds continued to sing and dart from tree to tree. Life around her went on, even though her own life was falling apart.

"The posse will want to know where the gold is."

"We never touched it." Bella remembered the three gold nuggets and flushed. "I mean, other than Andi taking those three nuggets. I meant to put them back, but Wayne found me before I could return them."

"That's probably a good thing."

"In what way?"

"If Wayne had followed you up there, Andria and I wouldn't have had a chance to follow. Wayne would be in charge of the treasure."

"They're going to blame Andi."

"Maybe. Maybe not."

Bella stared at him with confusion.

"The gold came from a heist committed several years back. I know Andi didn't have anything to do with it."

"How can you be so sure? The townspeople won't agree."

"I know because I used to ride with the gang that stole the gold."

Bella gaped at him. "You're tellin' me that you, an upstandin' Bible preachin' man, had something to do with a gold heist?"

"I haven't always been the *fine upstanding* man that you see today." His words were laced with sarcasm.

"I don't believe it." She stared at the handsome man before her. "What could you possibly have had to do with a gold heist?"

"I rode with a gang, a family gang, for years." Duncan shook his head. "Ever hear of the Marshalls?"

"I have."

"They're my brothers. Well, the gang was made up of me and my brothers." He scowled.

Bella knew the feeling. Once you knew right from wrong, you wondered how you could have possibly made the wrong choice for so long.

"I found out about God from a traveling preacher and decided to change my ways. But even before that, I'd started to question why we did what we did. I was the youngest of my brothers. Our way of life was all I knew. One day I slowed enough to see the pain on a victim's face. We hadn't hurt her, but we'd taken something precious from her. Her security. I couldn't get her pain out of my head. I knew that because of us, she'd have to live with fear for the rest of her life. I didn't want to ever see that look on another person's face."

Bella's heart went out to him. She understood what he was describing all too well. "I've seen that look. That moment when a person realizes that something they're going through is out of their control and that the circumstance will affect them for the rest of their life."

Duncan nodded, his face filled with pain. "That's it. I realized our actions lasted longer for the people involved than the few minutes it took us to do a heist. I told my brothers I wanted out, and they laughed. They couldn't imagine why I'd want to quit. They didn't understand why I'd even question what we'd always done. It was our way of life."

"What happened?"

"They cut me out and went through with the gold heist when I was out of town. When I realized what was going on, I rode as hard as I could to get back to them. They'd all been shot. Two of them were killed while doing the heist. One died at our family home. He made it back there, but I wasn't home to help him. The papers said all four were shot, but I never did find out what happened to my fourth brother, Danny."

"I think I know."

Duncan looked at her in surprise.

"Andria said there was a skeleton in with the gold."

"In the cave?"

"Yes."

Duncan nodded. "That would make sense. Danny made it to the cave but couldn't get any farther." A momentary look of defeat filled his eyes, and he paced a few steps away. "I've always hoped that he made it out of there, that he'd found medical help and would someday reappear. I'd hoped he'd also see the wrong in what they did and would come back a changed man. I guess I have to let that dream go."

"Well, we can't know for sure it's him. Not until you look things over."

"True. But I doubt that anyone else found the gold and left it there. It makes more sense that Danny made it there, a place he'd planned to meet up with the others, and that he died from his wounds."

"I'm so sorry." Bella wondered if she should have kept that part to herself, but figured he'd know soon enough anyway.

She looked up to see him studying her.

"You're hurt."

Bella looked down at her wrists. Doc had cleaned the wounds and bandaged them. "Just a little. The cuts aren't deep. They'll heal quickly."

"I'm sorry I wasn't there."

"You couldn't have known." Bella smiled, not used to the compassion. She figured she could settle down with a man like Duncan after all.

"We'll need to go into town and tell them everything we've shared with each other."

"I know." Bella bit her lip. "What do you think they'll make of us—Andria and me? Will they want justice served in full?"

Duncan reached forward and tucked a strand of Bella's hair behind her ear. "I think, after they hear what we have to say, they'll realize we all were victims of our families and that you and Andria did what you had to, in order to survive."

"We?"

He pointed from his chest to hers. "We. I intend to share my past with the townspeople. I've built myself up to a position of respect with them. I prayed daily that my past would never catch up with me. My whole ministry was about being genuine with my parishioners, yet I kept my past from them. I always felt something was missing from my ministry but couldn't put my finger on what was wrong."

"I don't want you to bring all this up on our account."

He smiled at her. "It's time I came clean with the whole sordid story. I don't think it'll matter to my believers. They'll welcome the idea that I'm no different than they are. And trust me, I know all their secrets and sins."

Bella sighed. "I wish none of this had ever happened."

"Bella." Duncan smiled and pulled her into his arms. "God doesn't make mistakes. He's had a purpose for you from the very beginning. He'll use your past to help others in the future. You'll be able to give hope and compassion to whoever He puts in your path."

"You're sure?"

"I am." He tilted her chin up so she had to look him in the eyes. His brown eyes were filled with love. "We'll go into town, we'll share what we've been through, and I feel sure that you and Andria will be set free. Charlie will face charges for his part in things, but I think he'll come around. Wayne will be in longer, but I pray we can reach him with patience and perseverance."

"I certainly hope so." Bella couldn't take her eyes off Duncan. His warm breath fanned her face. Her heart fluttered at his closeness.

"And you and I. . ." His words drifted off as he smiled. "You and I will marry and live happily ever after."

"We will?" Her voice came out in a squeak. She'd gone from confident outlaw to giddy female in a moment's time.

"We will," he whispered. He leaned forward and claimed her lips, sealing his promise with a kiss.

A Letter To Our Readers

Dear Reader:
In order that we might better contribute to your reading enjoyment, we would appreciate your taking a few minutes to respond to the following questions. We welcome your comments and read each form and letter we receive. When completed, please return to the following:

Fiction Editor
Heartsong Presents
PO Box 719
Uhrichsville, Ohio 44683

1. Did you enjoy reading *The Reluctant Outlaw* by Paige Winship Dooly?
   ❑ Very much! I would like to see more books by this author!
   ❑ Moderately. I would have enjoyed it more if

   _____

   _____

   _____

2. Are you a member of **Heartsong Presents**? ❑ Yes ❑ No
   If no, where did you purchase this book? _____

   _____

3. How would you rate, on a scale from 1 (poor) to 5 (superior), the cover design? _____

4. On a scale from 1 (poor) to 10 (superior), please rate the following elements.

   ____ Heroine   ____ Plot
   ____ Hero   ____ Inspirational theme
   ____ Setting   ____ Secondary characters

5. These characters were special because? _____

_____

_____

6. How has this book inspired your life? _____

_____

_____

7. What settings would you like to see covered in future
   Heartsong Presents books? _____

_____

_____

8. What are some inspirational themes you would like to see
   treated in future books? _____

_____

_____

9. Would you be interested in reading other **Heartsong
   Presents** titles? ❑ Yes ❑ No

10. Please check your age range:
    ❑ Under 18   ❑ 18-24
    ❑ 25-34   ❑ 35-45
    ❑ 46-55   ❑ Over 55

Name _____

Occupation _____

Address _____

City, State, Zip _____

E-mail _____

Heart♥ng

HEARTSONG PRESENTS TITLES AVAILABLE NOW:

(If ordering from this page, please remember to include it with the order form.)

Presents

Great Inspirational Romance
at a Great Price!

Heartsong Presents Heartsong Presents books are inspirational romances in contemporary and historical settings, designed to give you an enjoyable, spirit-lifting reading experience. You can choose wonderfully written titles from some of today's best authors like Wanda E. Brunstetter, Mary Connealy, Susan Page Davis, Cathy Marie Hake, Joyce Livingston, and many others.

When ordering quantities less than six, above titles are $3.99 each.
Not all titles may be available at time of order.